THE THANKSGIVING
HOOKUP

by

J. Sterling

Thank you for purchasing this book.

Sign up for my newsletter to get emails about new releases, upcoming releases, and special price promotions:

NEWSLETTER

Come join my private reader group on Facebook for giveaways:

PRIVATE READER GROUP

facebook.com/groups/ThePerfectGameChangerGroup

Other Books by J. Sterling

Bitter Rivals—an enemies to lovers romance

Dear Heart, I Hate You

10 Years Later—A Second Chance Romance

In Dreams—a new adult college romance

Chance Encounters—a coming-of-age story

THE GAME SERIES

The Perfect Game—Book One

The Game Changer—Book Two

The Sweetest Game—Book Three

The Other Game (Dean Carter)—Book Four

THE PLAYBOY SERIAL

Avoiding the Playboy—Episode #1

Resisting the Playboy—Episode #2

Wanting the Playboy—Episode #3

THE CELEBRITY SERIES

Seeing Stars—Madison & Walker

Breaking Stars—Paige & Tatum

Losing Stars—Quinn & Ryson

THE FISHER BROTHERS SERIES
No Bad Days—a New Adult, Second Chance Romance
Guy Hater—an Emotional Love story
Adios Pantalones—a Single Mom Romance
Happy Ending

THE BOYS OF BASEBALL
(THE NEXT GENERATION OF
FULLTON STATE BASEBALL PLAYERS)
The Ninth Inning—Cole Anders
Behind the Plate—Chance Carter
Safe at First—Mac Davies

FUN FOR THE HOLIDAYS
(A COLLECTION OF STAND-ALONE NOVELS
WITH HOLIDAY-BASED THEMES)
Kissing my Co-worker
Dumped for Valentine's
My Week with the Prince
Fools in Love
Spring's Second Chance
Don't Marry Him
Summer Lovin'
Flirting with Sunshine
Falling for the Boss
Tricked by my Ex
The Thanksgiving Hookup
Christmas with Saint

THE MOST ANNOYING PILOT

SKY

*O*H, *PLEASE, GOD, no*, I grumbled under my breath as I neared the departure gate at the terminal, rolling my carry-on behind me.

River Santos, the world's cockiest and most gorgeous captain, was sitting in one of the chairs, alerting me to the fact that he would be flying our plane tonight. I almost started bargaining with the Almighty, asking for anyone but River to take the controls, but knew it would be no use.

The airport was already tumultuous enough. An impending storm had canceled multiple flights, and the aftermath was all around me in the form of screaming babies and frustrated passengers just trying to get home. I knew that if our plane actually got cleared to take off, it was going to be a bumpy ride. In more ways than one.

I took the precious few moments before River noticed me nearing to really study him. It wasn't something I usually allowed myself to do. Mostly because he was always paying attention to us flight attendants and trying to eavesdrop on our conversations. We were a gossipy bunch. But if the pilots didn't give us such good material to work with, then we'd have nothing to talk about. Basically, it was their own faults that they were our favorite topics of discussion.

River used to date my friend and fellow flight attendant Stacy. At least, that was what she always told me. But that was before I started working for the airline. He was the first pilot Stacy had warned me about, telling me that he was as typical as they came. A man-whore who slept with half the staff and left a trail of broken hearts in his wake, hers included.

She had told me to stay away from him. And me, being the good rule-following friend that I was, had listened to her. I didn't want to make things at work uncomfortable, and crossing that line with River would definitely do that.

Stacy clearly wasn't over him even though she claimed that she was. I saw the way she looked at him whenever they happened to cross paths and I was around. Her eyes lit up like he'd hung the moon and stars, and she acted like a lovestruck teenager, just waiting to be noticed.

Why is he so freaking hot? It's not fair.

Just watching him annoyed me. He looked so at ease, sitting in a sea of frantic people, lost in his own world, typing something on his phone. His pilot's hat was sitting in his lap, and his stupid dark hair was perfectly gelled into place, per usual. That man never had a bad hair day. It wasn't in his DNA—or in the gel he probably owned stock in.

I took two more steps, and I swore that man could feel whenever I was close to him. He looked up slowly, like we were in some kind of movie, his deep blue eyes roving up the length of my body until he reached my face. A smirk appeared.

"Well, well," he said before locking eyes with mine, stopping me in my tracks. "I get to have you tonight, Sky?"

I snapped my jaw shut and ground my teeth together,

attempting to stop whatever sarcastic remark was about to come out of my mouth. It was all in vain. I couldn't help it. River's existence made me snarky.

"You'll never get to have me," I sniped.

He gave me a wink before adding, "So you keep saying."

"At least I'm consistent."

"No, Sky. You're a challenge," he said before licking his lips, and I pretended not to be the least bit affected by that calculated move. "Men live for a challenge."

"Good thing I don't see any men around here then," I lied, glancing around the chaotic terminal to prove my point.

River laughed, a full-on attention-drawing howl, before pushing out of his seat and hovering above me. All six feet three of him. I held my breath as he leaned down, his lips inches from my ear.

"You're not my type anyway."

Thankfully, most everyone was distracted by all the cancellations and delays. On a normal day, whenever the flight crew was sitting at the gate, people couldn't help but pay attention to us. They were fascinated by our perceived lifestyle. I'd been asked more times than I could count how often I flew, where my favorite destination was, if I was allowed to date the passengers, and what I was doing when we landed.

My eyes pulled together as my embarrassment swelled. I was nothing if not quick-witted. "There is a god," I breathed out dramatically.

"It's cute how you pretend you don't want me."

"It's kind of psychotic how you think that I do. Are you sure you're fit to fly? I mean, here." I tapped the side of my head and made a face.

"Bet you'd love to see how fit I am." His dark blue eyes narrowed playfully, but I wasn't playing.

I shoved at his stupidly hard chest—of course it was probably perfect as well—and growled when he didn't move an inch. "Just stay away from me."

"Gladly." He grinned, and I hated the way he could make me feel like I was beneath him somehow.

River was like a roller coaster, taking me up in the air one second and plunging me toward the ground the next. It was jarring, but even I had to admit that a small part of me enjoyed our banter. His comebacks always kept me on my toes. Unlike the other pilots, who weren't even the least bit creative when it came to hitting on me.

I was just about to say something else to River when I felt a strong tap on my shoulder. I swung around, noticed one of our "senior mama's", and squealed.

"Oh! Carmella! I'm so happy to see you!"

I hadn't worked with her in months. Flight attendant life was that way sometimes. You could work with someone once and then never see them again while you crossed paths with others more regularly if you were lucky.

"How long has it been?" Her New York accent hit my ears, and I smiled in response to hearing it.

She had given me all kinds of tips and tricks when I was brand-new on the job. Like how to deal with drunk passengers without pissing them off and creating a scene (flirt) and how to avoid dating the pilots (don't flirt).

"Three months at least. Where have you been?" I asked because I'd flown this route a few times lately and she'd never been on it.

"Oh, everywhere, honestly. I'm a last-minute replacement. Someone called in sick, and I happened to end my route here. I'm hoping we actually take off. It's getting pretty bad out there." She glanced at River before extending her hand. "I'm sorry, have we met?"

"Stop it," he answered, his tone oozing with charm and sincerity. It sounded nothing like the way he talked to me. "Come here, you gorgeous thing, you."

He pulled her in for a hug, and I swore I heard her sigh out loud, her face instantly flushing against his jacket. This guy seemed to have that effect on everyone. Except me. River might be gorgeous, but he knew it. And guys like that were a danger to your heart.

"Do you just get handsomer with age?" Carmella asked River, her jet-black hair swaying as she turned to look at me. "He does, doesn't he?"

I rolled my eyes and grunted, "I wouldn't know."

Even though Carmella had told me point-blank that dating a pilot would only end in heartbreak, she always seemed to have a soft spot for River. Or at least the way he looked.

Carmella laughed. "Oh, honey, we all know. Everyone with eyes knows."

"Well, my eyes don't like looking at him."

Liar.

"River"—she tsked as she turned back to face him—"you didn't," she said without finishing.

We all knew what she was hinting at. That River and I had hooked up.

"Ew. No," I protested a little too emphatically at the same time River did.

"Not a chance," he said for additional emphasis, and I hated how ugly it made me feel.

It was one thing when I was the one dissing him, but every time he did it back to me in response, I hated him for it.

I know; I know. I'm a hypocrite. Still don't care.

"Mmhmm." She looked between us, her eyes narrowing as she reached for my arm and pulled me aside. "Sky, what did I tell you about the pilots?"

I threw my hands in the air. "We haven't. I didn't. I swear."

"But you want to." She tilted her head and studied me as I frowned.

"I most certainly do not."

I'd never do that to Stacy. She'd never forgive me.

Typical nine-to-five workplace romances were tricky enough, but romances in the air were another beast altogether. Not to mention the fact that all the warnings I'd received about the men who flew our planes had been pretty spot on. I'd done my best to avoid hooking up with any of them so far, not that it had been that difficult, honestly. Whenever a particularly handsy pilot was going to head out with the crew on a layover, I opted to stay in my hotel room instead. That had earned me the title slam-clicker. I didn't care about the name.

The last thing I wanted was to be a notch on a bedpost, or a number in a city, or embarrassed whenever we had to work together. And I definitely wouldn't want anyone to find out about it. That was the biggest issue—people in this industry always found out everything. There were no secrets. I knew more about my coworkers' sex life than I'd ever wanted to.

And don't get me started on the awkwardness. One time, a pilot had had his wife and his mistress on the same plane. His mistress had to serve drinks and food to the wife the entire time. To say it was one of the most uncomfortable situations for the rest of us would be an understatement. I remembered waiting for the shit to hit the fan the entire flight, bracing myself for a fight that, thankfully, never came. My stomach had been in knots until we landed and the flight attendant ran into the restroom in the back of the aircraft and threw up until all the passengers deplaned.

I watched as Carmella glanced back in River's direction before focusing on me again. "God knows I love that boy, but he's a heartbreaker."

"I know. I've heard all about it."

A loudspeaker in the gate crackled to life before announcing that we would begin boarding soon, and the waiting passengers all seemed to exhale in unison. I realized that they had all expected a cancellation announcement at any moment and were relieved that we'd be taking off. Glancing out the large windows, I saw the snow falling heavily. The sooner we took off, the sooner we'd be back on solid ground again.

"Ladies"—River appeared at our sides—"that's our cue."

"Where's your first officer?" I asked.

Even though it was a quick twenty-five-minute flight,

there were always two pilots. It was a safety protocol that all airlines followed.

River gave a head nod, and we all turned in time to see a first officer heading our direction, his suitcase in tow right behind him. I glanced at his left hand, noticing the absence of a ring there. But that didn't necessarily mean anything. Lots of pilots took their wedding rings off before a flight or during a layover. It never made any sense to me, to be honest. It wasn't like we wouldn't find out they were married eventually. Why did they always try to lie about it?

"I'm Chad," he said as he reached our little group, and we all took turns introducing ourselves.

"All right. Gang's all here," River announced, and we simultaneously reached for our credentials and headed toward the jet bridge like we owned the place.

THE SEXIEST FLIGHT ATTENDANT

RIVER

S KY CALLAHAN WAS the bane of my existence. Ever since our first flight together, she'd given me the dirtiest looks and been cold as ice toward me. The woman was always snarling or rolling her eyes like I disgusted her somehow. If this were anyone else, I would ask them straight up why they were upset with me before fixing it and mending fences. But I'd never done a damn thing to Sky, so I wasn't about to ask her shit. If she wanted to be a bitch to me, so be it. I'd be one right back.

I knew I hadn't done anything to deserve her ire, but I'd be lying if I said I didn't want to fuck her senseless anyway. I thought about it more times than I cared to admit. And the woman hated me, which was probably why she starred in my fantasies so often. Hate fucking could be hot. Not that I'd ever done it. Women didn't usually despise me so publicly. Or at all, to be honest.

Her personality was just as fire-filled as her red hair, and she had green eyes that dazzled like fucking emeralds anytime the light hit them just right. She challenged me at every turn. It was as infuriating as it was sexy. Sky was an absolute stunner, but she was also a stuck-up snob. If I made a comment about any topic on the planet, she asked me where I heard it or how I knew that my information was correct. She was like a walking fact-checker from CNN or something, always desperate to prove me wrong.

Most of the other flight attendants couldn't have cared less about the things I said. They were all too willing to screw on a layover, dropping me their room keys whenever we all hung out at the hotel bar or were enjoying a night out. Even the ones with boyfriends or husbands at home.

This industry didn't lend itself to the most faithful of people. And it wasn't just the pilots despite our reputations. I also didn't take the attached women up on their offers despite mine.

I never did much to dispel any of the things that were said about me. And trust me, there were a lot. Truthfully, it seemed like a waste of time. Did I fuck some of the women I worked with? Absolutely. As long as we were two single, consenting adults, I didn't see the problem. Also, I had stopped doing that shit over a year ago, but no one ever talked about that part.

It was all, *River screwed so-and-so in New Orleans during a layover.* Or, *Did you hear about River and so-and-so in the airport restroom?*

Truthfully, I didn't really care what people thought about my personal life, so I never corrected them or said anything to the contrary when I happened to overhear a falsity about me. It was none of their business anyway even though they all acted like it was.

My main focus was to be great at flying, stay out of trouble, and go on all the adventures that having this job afforded me. It really wasn't a good time to be a young guy hooking up with coworkers anyway. Too many things got misconstrued, and feelings were easily hurt, no matter how truthful or forthcoming you were beforehand.

Hurt feelings led to lawsuits.

I had watched it happen to a couple of my friends, and it scared the piss out of me. Which was why I had started keeping my dick in my pants at work.

Being an airline pilot had been my dream ever since a teacher had asked me what I wanted to be when I grew up. My father was one as well, and I wanted to be just like him. In the beginning, I worshipped him for it. He made it seem like the most exciting job anyone could ever have, and he always came home, bearing gifts from all the places he'd visited.

I never understood how messed up it all truly was. And I never realized when I was just a kid that my father was screwing all the women he introduced me to behind my mother's back. All I knew was that they were nice ladies who plied me with soda until my stomach hurt and always gave me a pair of those plastic wings I could put on my shirt.

Once I was old enough to start putting the pieces together, I felt awful for my mother. She deserved better.

I had told her more than once to leave him, but she always looked at me with sad eyes and asked, "But where would I go?"

Whenever anything went wrong in our family, our mother was the one my siblings and I ran to. We depended on her to always be there. She was our security blanket, the calm in the middle of the storm, always strong and steadfast. I'd never once considered her weak for staying married to my father even though I eventually hated him for it.

Those had been different times back then. Times when a woman was taught to look the other way when it came to her husband's indiscretions. As long as he was taking care of the family and providing for them financially, he was entitled to have a little fun on the side.

"Everyone cheats," the neighborhood women used to say as they commiserated together, drinking wine by the box.

So, yeah, I still wanted to be a pilot, but I no longer wanted to be like my father.

"Hello? River? Move. What are you doing? Staring at your reflection somewhere?"

Sky gave me a slight nudge against my back, and I realized that I'd stopped in the middle of the check-in counter, my badge still sitting on the scanner, while everyone stared.

"Thought you might want a little extra time to check me out from the back." I smirked, and her expression instantly soured.

"That's what you get for thinking."

"That mouth is going to get you in trouble one of these days." I gave her a nod before my eyes locked on to her lips and held. I imagined them wrapped around my cock. Hate sucking me right here in the middle of the terminal.

"Doubtful." She gave me a fake smile.

I refocused my attention away from Sky and back toward the flight I was about to pilot. Before stepping inside the plane, I tapped the top of it three times and once on each side of the doorway. It was tradition. Or superstition. Whatever you called it, I never flew without doing it.

"That makes me feel *very* secure," Sky mumbled from behind me, obviously judging.

"Don't you have a job to do?" I snapped, practically biting her head off, and I could tell that my response shocked her.

She walked away from me without saying another word.

When I headed into the cockpit, the first thing I noticed was how bad the weather was getting. The snow started falling harder, and the winds had definitely picked up, blowing the flakes at a harsh angle. If we were cleared to take off, no doubt we were going to be one of the last planes before they called it for the night.

Poking my head into the galley, I spotted Carmella and waved her over. "Let's get everyone on as quickly as possible so we can get out of here."

"That bad?" she asked.

"It's getting there," I answered honestly.

"Are you nervous?"

I grinned. "Me? Nah. It's just a little snow."

It wasn't a lie. We had a de-icing system that made the weather less of a challenge and helped keep us safe. The main issue when it came to a storm like this was visibility. And right now, I could still see. But that could change at any moment.

"What does make you nervous, Captain Santos?"

"Lightning," I answered without hesitation.

Lightning was a bitch. It was unpredictable and caused severe damage without any warning. Controls fried.

Things blew apart. Fires started. Hands down, that was the scariest weather to navigate.

"Oh, me too," Carmella agreed before shuddering.

"Let's get those passengers safely on board and get up in the air."

"You got it." She saluted, and I laughed.

WE LANDED SAFELY and just in time. As I had suspected, the airports in the area all started closing down, including the one we'd just flown out of. There was a blizzard blanketing the area, set to drop something like three feet of snow in twelve hours and not stopping for days. That was a lot of snow.

The visibility on the runway was almost at zero already. Sure, we had equipment to help us navigate once we were up in the air, but it wasn't safe to land or take off in these kinds of conditions. Safety was, after all, our first priority. Much to the passengers' chagrin. I understood their frustrations when it came to weather delays and cancellations, but it simply wasn't worth the risk.

No flight was worth dying over.

I grabbed my rollaboard from behind my seat and handed Chad his as I opened the cockpit door.

"That was gnarly," he said as we waited for the flight attendants to exit the aircraft before we got off ourselves.

I was always the last one to leave, and I walked up and down the aisles one last time to make sure no one was still on board. They never were, but I still liked to check. Another superstition, I guessed.

"What do you know about her?" Chad gave a nod in Sky's direction, and I felt my jealous nature start to rise even though he was almost a foot shorter than I was. Not that it meant a damn thing, but I was competitive and a dick sometimes and enjoyed the fact that I towered over him.

"She's mean," I said, hoping to steer him away from her.

He laughed. "Mean I can handle. Is she single?"

I shrugged. "Not sure. I think I heard her talking about a boyfriend and them taking a trip to Hawaii not that long ago," I lied through my teeth.

Sky was one hundred percent single, and I knew it. I stalked her social media whenever I got bored or needed some hate spank material and had yet to see her with a guy who stuck around for longer than three posts. Her stories were filled with places she had flown to, and she was always with other people on the crew, never with anyone romantically. I'd even gone so far as to watch her stories online even though I knew she'd be able to see that I had. Figured I'd own up to it if she called me out on it, which she hadn't done so far.

"That's too bad," he groaned, and I felt like I'd won. "Then again, he's not here, and I am."

"Not sure she's the type," I said, meaning that Sky wasn't the kind of girl to cheat when her made-up man wasn't around.

"They're all the type," Chad said with a wink, and I felt my lips turn up into a snarl.

"Not all of them," I said through gritted teeth. And not because he was making an insinuation about the entire female staff, but because he was making it about Sky. And for some reason, it pissed me the hell off. Apparently, I was the only one allowed to disrespect her.

Hypocrite.

"You mean to tell me you haven't bagged her? The

great Captain Santos has left some for the rest of us?"

I wanted to tell him that I'd had her more times than I could count, but I didn't want to lie about something like that. "She's not my type."

He let out a howl before slapping me on the shoulder. "You're joking. You know what they say about redheads, right?"

"Yeah, that they're all psycho."

Chad made a face before adding, "Yeah, they do say that. But they also say that they're wild in the sack, man. Best sex you'll ever have is with a redhead."

"And then they'll burn your house down after doing it."

"Worth it," he said.

I realized that I was starting to sweat; I was getting so amped up.

This guy was going to be a problem.

When we stepped out of the jet bridge and into the terminal, it was like a ghost town. All of the restaurants and stores were closed, and only a handful of people were still inside, sleeping on the ground, using their balled-up sweatshirts as pillows. It was going to be a long few days for them if they stayed here the whole time.

Then again, where were people supposed to go when all the hotels were sold out and the rental agencies were out of cars? Options became extremely limited during a storm like this. Sometimes, staying put was the safest choice even if it felt like the most inconvenient and uncomfortable one at the time.

"How long did they say the airport was closing for?" Sky stopped walking and directed her question at both me and Chad, her green eyes volleying between us.

I answered before he could, "At least two days."

"So, we're stuck here?"

"Happy Thanksgiving to us," Carmella added with a frown, and I knew then that she had planned on spending the holiday with her family back in New York.

I forgot that people did things like that—actually requested holidays off to be with their loved ones. I was so used to not being around relatives on those days, what with the busy travel schedule and bonus pay, that it slipped my mind that others might not feel the same way.

Glancing at Sky, I realized that she looked a little sad. Maybe she did have a boyfriend I didn't know about.

"Did you have plans?" I asked her sincerely, actually trying to be nice for once.

I felt a little bad that she'd be missing out on them.

"Why? Did you want to ruin them?"

And just like that, I didn't feel bad anymore.

STUCK TOGETHER

SKY

I HAD INTENDED to give River a nice and normal response, but my brain had other ideas. It was as though once Stacy had warned me about the kind of man River was, I couldn't see him any other way. And all the things I'd heard about him since hadn't helped. He slept around, but didn't get serious with anyone. River fit the mold of a playboy pilot to a T. Hell, he'd probably been the one they made the mold after.

In my mind, River had somehow morphed into every guy I'd crossed paths with during my college years. The kind who lied to get what they wanted from a girl and manipulated her into thinking she was special when she wasn't. I'd fallen for the act more times than I could count back then, hating myself each and every time after. I refused to fall for it at this stage of my life. I knew they always said that men matured slower than women, but I was starting to think that some didn't mature at all.

The four of us walked through the airport toward our designated pickup area, where we'd load up in a van waiting to take us to our hotel. I hoped it was nice and that the room service would be operational, especially since we'd be stuck there for the next few days.

Staring at the storm outside the airport windows, I knew I wouldn't be getting back to Florida anytime soon. That much was clear. My mom was going to be so disappointed. For once, I had actually planned on being home with her, my brother, and my niece for Thanksgiving. I'd missed the last three since I'd started working for the airline, much to her displeasure. I actually enjoyed being in a new city each year, trying to find turkey with my friends from the crew. It had become a tradition of sorts, and I looked forward to it. Plus, the holiday pay was a nice bonus.

But this year, my mom had convinced me to come

home. Mostly because my brother and his family would be at their in-laws for Christmas, so if we didn't have Thanksgiving together, then who knew when I'd see them again? Apparently, I was always working, and my niece was getting bigger by the day, destined to forget all about her auntie Sky if I didn't come around. I didn't want that to happen, so I had requested the time off.

We all neared the exit, and I grabbed my jacket, buttoning it up tight as I braced for the cold that I was certain would hit me the second we stepped outside. I was a Florida girl through and through. Humidity I could handle. But the snow and frozen ice chunks that blew through the wind? Those always seemed to chill my bones hard and fast. I never quite got warm enough.

"Ready?" Chad asked as we got even closer toward the exit doors. "The van's right there." He pointed at it, and we all nodded, ready to hand the driver our luggage as quickly as possible.

Once we were situated inside the van, the driver flashed us a concerned look. "I'm really hoping we don't get stuck on the way there," he said, and my eyes widened.

"What? You think we'll get stuck?" The question

slipped through my lips.

Thanksgiving in a hotel with River wasn't exactly my idea of a great time, but being stuck on the side of a road in a snowed-in van sounded even less appealing. I saw it all play out in my head. River would try to convince me to have sex with him.

One for the road, he'd say. He'd beg. He wouldn't stop talking about it.

Then, we'd die with his frozen penis inside my vagina, and that was how people would find us. Stuck together forever.

They'd write that we were in love. Or that we were trying to stay alive by sharing our body heat. When the truth would be that I was giving him a pity fuck so he'd finally stop talking and shut up for once.

"We should be all right, but we really need to go," the driver answered.

"Are we waiting on anyone else?" River asked, and the driver shook his head. "Let's hit it," he said before smacking the back of the seat with his palm.

Pulling out my cell phone, I typed out a quick text to my mom, letting her know that I was snowed in and wouldn't be making it for Thanksgiving. She was definitely asleep at this hour, but it was better I let her know sooner rather than later. She'd wake up to the message and no doubt call me about it instead of texting back a response. I needed to remember to put my phone on silent once I got checked in and settled in my room for the night. The last thing I needed was to be woken up at some ungodly hour, just to be yelled at.

THANK GOD THE only scary thing about the drive was how slow we had to go. The roads were slippery, and the visibility was awful. Near whiteout conditions at times, which were definitely only going to get worse as the night wore on. It took us over an hour to get to a hotel that was typically fifteen minutes away, at most. Seeing the red neon lights through the falling snow made me smile.

We'd made it.

I couldn't wait to take a long, hot bath and hoped that my room had a tub. We piled out of the van, thanked the driver, grabbed our bags, maneuvered through the double doors, and walked up to the front counter, bringing in clumps of snow with us.

The first thing I noticed was how many people were up at this hour and hanging out. It seemed like every single corner and table was filled with families and people on their laptops. When I saw trays of food still being delivered, I breathed out a sigh of relief. I was hungry and had only packed a few light snacks. Nothing that would actually settle my grumbling stomach. And since our flight had been so short, we hadn't had anything that I could take from the galley. No pretzels, no peanuts, no cookies. Nada.

"I'm so happy to see that food," Carmella whispered toward me as the woman at the check-in counter typed frantically on her keyboard, working some sort of magic with her fingers, like they always seemed to do.

"I want to order one of everything," I said with a laugh.

I signed the check-in sheet that the airline had called over. It had each one of our four names listed with the checkout date noted as *pending*. Never a good sign.

"Please tell me I have a bathtub," I mumbled toward the hotel employee, who was still typing on her computer as she grinned to herself.

"All your rooms do. You actually got the last four. We're all sold out," she said before handing me a single key card. "Here you go. You're all on the same floor."

"How about we head to our rooms, change, and meet back down here in ten?"

It was River who was asking. I hadn't expected it or even considered the fact that everyone would want to hang out together. Weren't they exhausted like I was? Didn't they want to soak in a long, hot bubble bath until the water turned cold?

"Is the bar still open?" Chad asked.

"It's open until the crowd starts to die down," the employee answered.

"Really?" I asked.

"We typically close around eleven, but the bartender decided to stay and keep the bar open He lives about an hour away, so he's stuck here too."

"That was nice of him," I said as I exhaled.

"Meet in ten?" River pushed once more, and we all agreed—me begrudgingly—as we headed toward the bank of waiting elevators.

The doors opened with a thud, and we all stepped inside as Carmella swiped her room key and promptly pressed the seven button.

"We are all on seven, right?" she asked, and we all said, "Yes."

When I stepped off, my eyes searched for the signs on the wall that would direct me toward my room. "I'm this way." I gave a head nod toward the right.

"I'm the opposite," Carmella said with a nod of her own.

"Me too," Chad said.

I wasn't sure which one of us he was referring to, but I saw him following in Carmella's direction.

I started walking and felt River's presence close behind me. He kept his distance as I read off the numbers next to the doors in search of mine.

"I'm here," I said as I stopped abruptly, and River stood right next to me, his suitcase at his side.

"Me too."

"What? We're not sharing a room." I knew my voice sounded horrified, but if he thought I was sharing a room with him, he had another thing coming.

"I'm in the one next to you, apparently." He pointed at

the door right next to my own that I hadn't even noticed until now.

"Adjoining rooms? Did you ask for that?" I asked accusingly.

"Only in your dreams, sweetheart."

"More like nightmares," I growled before swiping my key and pushing inside, locking River out.

I heard him though. Moving around in the room next to mine before I noticed the door between our walls. I double-checked my side to make sure it was locked before I tossed my suitcase on top of my king-size bed and unzipped it.

The first thing I did was unpack all of my bathroom essentials. I knew that most people just dropped their makeup bag on the counter and lived out of it, but I wasn't one of them. I needed all of my hair and face stuff organized. But only those things. My clothes usually stayed inside my suitcase unless we were on a long layover and I had dresses that needed to be hung up in the closet.

Grabbing my toiletry bag, I carried it into the bathroom and smiled at the tub. "I'm coming for you later," I warned before I started pulling out my things and setting them on top of the counter.

Night creams and face wash on one side. Makeup, primer, and sunscreen on the other. Brush and hair products near the blow-dryer. Toothbrush, toothpaste, makeup remover, and a fresh washcloth right next to the faucet.

A loud knock scared me half to death, and I jumped before looking at my reflection. I looked like ass. My hair, which had been in a perfect ponytail when I started this morning, now had strands of red blown all over, sticking out like I'd stuck my finger in a light socket.

Another knock.

That wasn't my front door. Walking to the adjoining door, I unlocked it and pulled it open to see River standing there in jeans and a black T-shirt, his hand in the air, poised to knock again. No man should be that sexy and that aware of it.

"What do you want?"

His eyes looked at me, and he shook his head in disapproval. "You're not ready."

"I was unpacking."

He laughed. At me. "Unpacking? Really?"

I snarled, and he quickly backtracked.

"Can you get changed so we can go? They're already downstairs, looking for a table."

"You don't have to wait for me. I'm a big girl. I can meet you down there."

He leaned close to me, like he'd done in the airport earlier, but this time, his cologne was fresh, and it wafted into my senses, invading them completely. I had to stop myself from closing my eyes and inhaling.

"Might want to brush your hair first."

"Oh my God. You're such a jerk." I shoved at him, trying in vain to get him back on his side of the wall so I could slam the door in his face and never open it again.

"Meet you down there then," he said before closing *his* door first.

I stood there like a fool, staring at it, stewing.

I hated River Santos and his stupid cologne.

COLD PIZZA IS THE ONLY RIGHT ANSWER

RIVER

SKY EXITED THE elevator shortly after I did, hair brushed to fucking perfection. It looked as soft as silk, and I knew that what I'd said bothered her. Good. I liked knowing I got a rise out of her. It seemed only fair when all she seemed to do was ruffle my feathers whenever we crossed paths.

"Sky." Chad waved an arm in the air, gaining her attention.

When she neared, he stood up and pulled out a barstool for her.

Her eyes met mine, the fire still brewing behind them.

"A gentleman? How rare," she said, looking right at me as she spoke the words.

Gentleman, my ass.

Chad just wanted to fuck her so he could say he did. Especially now that he knew I hadn't. I should have lied and told him we'd hooked up before. Maybe then he wouldn't be so hell-bent on having her.

"Okay, the bartender's name is Raul. He's a sweetheart. Has no plans on closing anytime soon and said the kitchen's still open," Carmella said as she handed both me and Sky a menu.

"Making friends already, Carm?" I opened mine and started perusing the main courses.

She shrugged. "I like meeting new people. Especially when I'm not serving them."

"Amen to that," Sky added with an enthusiastic nod, her eyes glued to the menu.

The two of them had to deal with the passenger's way more than I ever did. The most interaction I had was greeting them and making an announcement or two. I wasn't the one they treated like a glorified hostess in the sky, like my sole purpose was to serve. Flight attendants were on board for safety purposes, not drink-serving ones.

"I wouldn't trade places with you girls for anything," I said right as Raul appeared, looking a little tired, but still smiling through it.

"Evening. Can I get you all something to drink?" His eyes roved around the four of us as he waited for our response.

I actually wasn't a big drinker. A beer or two was one thing, but getting full-on hammered usually left me feeling pretty shitty. And no matter how hard I hit the gym after to rid myself of the toxins, it never quite worked. I still felt like ass for a whole day while my body tried to recover. It wasn't worth it.

"I'll take a local beer," I said, and Raul nodded before I added, "Not an IPA."

"Gotcha," he said with a grin and an approving nod.

I listened as Chad ordered a double vodka with a splash of soda and a lime, and Carmella and Sky each ordered a glass of red wine. It looked like Chad would be the only one drunk tonight if he kept that drink order up. Better him than me. Raul disappeared before showing back up crazy fast, balancing our four drinks on a tray as he handed them out.

"Would you like to order food? I'm not sure how long the kitchen will stay open, so I'd get an order in sooner rather than later."

We all ordered meals like we weren't sure when we'd get the chance to eat again, and it made me laugh, just listening to the amount of food. Sky ordered a whole pizza for herself, and I shot her a look.

"What? I can bring the leftovers back to my room and eat them for breakfast," she explained.

"Cold or reheated?" I asked because there was only one correct answer.

"Cold. Reheated is nasty," she said, making a face, and I gave her a thumbs-up.

"No," Chad interjected. "Cold pizza is disgusting."

"Agree to disagree." She gave him a sweet smile, her eyes lingering on his face for far too long for my liking.

I felt the usually tight reins of my control starting to unravel.

"He's right." Carmella inserted her opinion on the matter, and, well, she was wrong too. "Cold pizza is unacceptable."

Sky shook her head. "You will never convince me that there's anything better than cold pizza straight out of the fridge in the morning."

"Sky's right," I said, ending the debate. "Cold. Right out of the fridge. Nothing better. End of."

"No. You're both wrong. Sorry, but you're wrong. Maybe it's 'cause I'm from New York, but I just can't agree with this blasphemy." Chad took a healthy swig of his drink without wincing.

I was never the kind of person who could drink straight vodka. It tasted like rubbing alcohol to me. Now, tequila, on the other hand … that had always been my drink of choice, and I could drink it straight with the best of them. But that seemed like a lifetime ago.

"You're from New York?" Carmella's face lit up like she was about to ask Chad if she could adopt him for Christmas.

"Yeah." Chad gave a shrug.

"What part? I'm from the Bronx," Carmella said, her accent thick and proud. "Go Yankees," she added, and we all laughed because it was so random. Not that she would like the Yankees, but that she'd bring up baseball.

Chad failed to respond, and Carmella waved her hand at him, trying to get him to spit it out.

I had no idea why he was so hesitant until he finally answered, "The Hamptons."

I threw my head back and whistled. "I didn't know anyone was actually *from* there. I thought it was just a place where rich people vacationed in the summer."

"I did too," Sky added with a wince. "Is that offensive to say?"

Chad laughed. "Not at all. I know that most people don't know much about it, except for what they read and hear on TV. But it's a real place, where you can live full-time and grow up and go to high school."

"It sounds fancy," Sky said, her eyes wide, and Carmella nodded.

"It is," Carmella said before Chad could disagree.

He downed the rest of his drink before signaling to Raul that he'd like another. The rest of us had barely even touched ours.

"Where are you two from?" Chad asked, trying to steer the conversation away from his fancy Hamptons upbringing.

"Florida," Sky and I both said at the same time, our voices echoing loudly in the bar area.

My eyes widened as I shook my head at her. "You're from Florida? What part?"

How hadn't I known that?

"You first," she said, her expression untrusting, like I might be lying about where I was from.

"Miami," I said, my Cuban accent coming out the same way that Carmella's seemed to when she talked about her home.

"It all makes so much sense now," Sky said, and I felt myself growing defensive.

I loved my hometown and wouldn't tolerate anything bad being said about it. Especially not from her.

"What does that mean?" I asked, my tone dead serious.

"You look like you belong in Miami. It suits you."

"How so?" I pushed, wanting to hear how she saw me. I didn't care that anyone else was around, listening to her judgment about me.

Sky laughed. "The player lifestyle. Beautiful women at your fingertips. The clubs and beaches as your playground and you're the king of it all."

I mean, she wasn't necessarily wrong, but I didn't feel like admitting that to her anytime soon.

"What part are you from?"

"Sarasota," she said, and now, it was my turn to judge.

"And it suddenly makes so much sense," I said, mocking her.

"Really?" she said sarcastically, but I was dead serious.

"Yeah. You're stuck-up and a brat. I bet you have a yacht," I said, and Chad laughed while Carmella sucked in a breath so quickly that it made a squeaking sound.

"Do you have a yacht?" Carmella asked, her voice filled with surprise.

"I do not have a yacht," Sky yelled as she narrowed her eyes at me. "And I'm not stuck-up. I just don't like you."

"Oh, sorry." I lifted one hand in the air. "I meant, your daddy has a yacht."

I was being an asshole, but it seemed fair. She had made so many judgments about me based on where I'd come from, so I wanted to do the same. Plus, it wasn't my fault that I was right.

"My dad's dead," Sky said.

Carmella inhaled another breath that squeaked before mumbling some words that sounded like a quick prayer and apology on my behalf.

"Nice job," Chad whispered as he leaned toward me.

My heart sank. "Hey, I'm sorry, Sky. I didn't know."

She waved me off. "It's fine. But my family doesn't have a yacht."

"Mine does." Chad shrugged as Raul deposited another drink in front of him, and we all laughed.

Of course this guy had a freaking yacht. I should have put it together that his arrogant, entitled ass was loaded, but I hadn't.

I glanced across the table at Sky and realized that she was watching Chad, curiosity in her eyes. Maybe she liked her guys rich … and short. Chad was both of those things. I was neither of them.

"I was going to see if the trains were running." Chad motioned toward Carmella, and she reached for her phone and started typing frantically.

"That would be ideal. I didn't even think about that," she breathed out as she continued tapping.

"What are you guys talking about?" Sky asked, thankful to be immersed in a new topic. "Amtrak?"

"If the trains are running, we could get home. Or at least pretty damn close to it," Chad said.

"But the airport's closed for at least two days." Sky was clearly confused, and I understood why. Logically, it made sense that if a runway couldn't open for planes, then train tracks should be closed as well. "That's what you said, right, River?"

"Trains are different. Crews can plow the snow from the tracks if it's too high, and then they attach a plow to the front of the engine for light clearing. If they can get the snow off the tracks safely, the train can still run. It just sometimes goes a lot slower than normal, but it still goes," I explained to her, and her mouth formed an O.

I waited for her to call me out, question all the things I had just told her, like she usually did, but she didn't. She just sat there, staring at Chad like he was the most fascinating thing in the hotel bar, and I had no idea why. He didn't seem like her type.

I didn't like what I was witnessing one bit, and I was about to fucking lose it.

ICE CREAM CHAD

SKY

I COULDN'T STOP staring at *Chad from the Hamptons*. There was something so familiar about him, and I couldn't place it. But now that I was sure I knew him from somewhere, I couldn't stop myself from watching his mannerisms and facial expressions.

Each time I stopped my quiet sleuthing and glanced at River, he was glaring at me. I rolled my eyes and shook my head, but he wouldn't look away. He sat there, analyzing me, while I did the same to someone else. Only River didn't look at all happy about it. My cell phone pinged out a notification, and I glanced down to see that someone had commented on one of my latest videos online.

That was when it hit me.

I did a quick search, typing in a hashtag and watching one quick clip to confirm my suspicions before saying anything.

"Oh my God, you're Ice Cream Chad, aren't you?"

Now that I'd placed his face with the once-trending hashtag from years ago, I couldn't unsee it. I knew I was right whether or not he admitted it. The proof was literally in my hand, on my phone screen.

"He's what?" River asked, his eyes pulled together with his confusion.

I bet he hated feeling left out. River was probably always included in everything. Poor baby.

"Ice Cream Chad. It is you, isn't it? I knew you looked familiar, but I couldn't figure out from where." I couldn't stop myself from talking, laughter creeping out with my words, while Chad looked downright horrified, most likely wishing that I would shut up.

"What the hell are you talking about? Are you drunk?" River questioned, his tone dripping with utter annoyance.

"No, I'm not drunk," I snapped.

"I'm a little lost myself." Carmella held her wineglass in the air before taking another drink of it and almost finishing it off.

I shook my head before blowing out an annoyed breath. "It's a TikTok thing," I said, as if that explained everything.

Although to most people, it would have. Apparently, River wasn't most people.

"You have TikTok?" River asked, his tone beyond rude. Like my having that particular app made me less respectable somehow.

"Everyone has TikTok," I said, sounding just as judgmental in return.

"I don't," he said.

"How shocking." The sarcasm dripped from my lips. "It's because you're no fun."

"I'm fun," he argued.

"Clearly."

"You're telling me that TikTok is fun? I thought it was all drama and angry people yelling about politics."

"What?" A laugh escaped me. "I've never even seen a single political video," I said before adding, "I have a carefully curated feed that only brings me joy."

It was true. I was extremely intentional with the videos I liked or commented on. That way, the app kept delivering more of what made me happy and less of the drama that tended to fill everyone else's pages. All it had taken was one "like" on an Ice Cream Chad post, and I had gone down the rabbit hole, getting updates and opinions each time I logged in.

"You have a … carefully curated … *what*?" River coughed as he shook his head.

He was completely lost, and I had to admit that it made me happy to know that he was this clueless about something so popular and well known. The guy seemed to know something about every topic and was always spouting off his knowledge about it whenever he had the chance.

"Someone please tell me what Ice Cream Chad is because it sounds yummy," Carmella said, and I let out another quick laugh.

Chad's cheeks were red, and it stopped me from spilling the details before I even got started. This was something that had trended online years ago, but it had been a huge deal back then. The story had made the news and gossip outlets. If I remembered correctly, multiple women had spoken up, and even though they had identified Chad and pinpointed exactly who he was, he'd never made a statement.

"It's okay. You can tell them. They're just going to look it up online at this point if you don't," Chad said before finishing off his vodka and signaling Raul for a third.

"He's not wrong," River said because he was obviously going to do just that if I didn't.

I probably would have done the same thing.

Now, I felt a little bad for putting the pieces together and placing Chad's face in front of everyone. I was sure this wasn't something he was proud of and that he'd hoped he could finally leave it all behind at some point, but online fame followed people in weird ways. It was never really gone; it only snoozed silently in the archives, waiting to be dug up and brought to life again.

"I feel bad," I said, looking only at Chad. "I shouldn't have said anything."

He shook his head as Raul delivered his drink and let us know our food would be ready shortly. "Don't. I didn't care then, and I don't care now. It is what it is."

Well, okay then.

Here I was, thinking that he'd be remorseful or morti-fied, but he wasn't. His face was probably red from all the alcohol, not embarrassment, like I'd presumed.

"All right. Well, Chad here got famous on TikTok for dating a bunch of women at the same time and then ghosting them for no reason."

"Wait. What's ghosting again?" Carmella asked, her eyes pulled together. "When they disappear, right?"

"Yeah." I nodded. "It's when a guy"—I looked point-edly at River—"or girl just basically drops off the face of the earth and never talks to you again after dating you. They ignore your calls, your texts, everything."

"Why are you looking at *me* like that?" River asked, and I figured it was obvious, considering that he'd done just that to Stacy after hooking up with her.

"Figured you were familiar with the term."

"I obviously know what ghosting is," he said before focusing on Chad, "but how'd you get 'famous' for that?" River made air quotes around the word, clearly not understanding the power of social media or a group of scorned women online who bonded over their mutual distaste for the same man.

"One girl posted about him on the app, and it went viral. Her comment section exploded with similar stories. Next thing you knew, there were literally hundreds of videos about Ice Cream Chad here and how he dated them for weeks before disappearing and never talking to them again."

"But why the ice cream part?" Carmella shook her head, trying to figure out something that seemingly made no sense from the outside.

"Because that's where I worked. At my family's ice cream shop in the Hamptons."

"You met a bunch of women at an ice cream shop?" River questioned, sounding more than a little skeptical.

"No. I met them online. But then I'd bring them all their favorite ice cream flavor from the store on our first date." Chad sounded almost proud of himself, like he had been so clever to think of that little trick.

"You did the same thing for each woman?" River smacked the table with his hand, like this was too much for him to believe. "And you didn't think you'd get caught?"

Chad shrugged a shoulder. "They were tourists. Only in town for a weekend or a week at a time. There's so many people coming and going in the Hamptons in the summer. It's a constant revolving door of hot, single women."

"But everyone found out who you were and what you were doing." I tried to remind him that his behavior hadn't been cool then, and it certainly wasn't cool now.

"Yeah. But by that point, I'd been doing it for two and a half summers. It was time to move on. Try something new."

Chad had learned nothing from his online shaming. Men could be a pretty disappointing species at times, and Chad was living proof of that.

"So, one video ruined it all?" Carmella asked, still trying to connect all the dots.

I nodded. "That first video got a lot of attention, and it led to hundreds more. Girls were crying. Some were angry. Some were embarrassed. People started showing up at the ice cream shop, doing live video feeds, all in search of Chad," I said, filling in more of the blanks because I had been super invested in the story for a while and knew way too much about it.

"They showed up, filming? Did anyone actually find you while they were doing that? What happened after?" Carmella finished off her wine, her focus solely on Chad, waiting for him to respond.

Chad blew out a breath. "It was a total shit show. I had to hide out until the season ended. My parents were harassed online and in person multiple times a day. That was the only part I felt bad about."

"Wait." I put up a hand. "*That* was the only part you felt bad about?"

Chad looked at me like I was the crazy one. "Well, yeah. My parents didn't do anything to deserve all the hate that got thrown their way. And honestly, neither did I."

The three of us laughed and made sounds as Chad quickly presented his defense before we could say another word.

"No, really. I mean it. Listen." He made eye contact with the three of us before he continued, "What did I do wrong? Date a bunch of women looking to have a fling with a rich guy from the Hamptons? Bring them ice cream and then stop talking to them after whatever we were doing ran its course or they left town? I never promised anyone forever. Never said we were exclusive or even dating. It was a hookup site, and I hooked up."

"But you were sleeping with multiple women at the same time," I said, trying to prove some kind of moral point.

"Yeah, I was. But so were they as far as I knew."

River cleared his throat, and I focused my attention on him. "I'm not sure Chad's the bad guy here. Sounds like he pissed off the wrong woman, is all."

"Seriously? You're defending this?" I sounded far more disgusted than I actually felt.

If it was true, I kind of understood what Chad was saying. *I just didn't like it.* I wouldn't want it happening to me, and hearing River take his side on the matter felt like some kind of betrayal.

Not that it made any kind of sense.

I hated River. Of course he'd side with Chad on this. They were two peas in a pod when it came to women. Dating whoever they wanted with no regard for anyone's feelings aside from their own.

"I'm just saying that I understand it. He dated multiple women. Who were most likely doing the same thing. I'm not victim blaming or saying that anyone who got hurt by him deserved it. Just saying, after hearing his perspective, it might not be so black and white."

Chad put a hand in the air for a high five, but River only looked at it before giving him a nod. Chad put his hand down.

"You get it, man, because you do the same thing," Chad added.

"I do not do the same thing," River challenged.

I choked on my drink because he kind of did, but I didn't feel like bringing that fact up for debate. There would be no winning, only more arguing, and I was exhausted, just thinking about it. Males and females didn't typically see things through the same set of eyes, and they definitely did not feel with the same emotions.

"Did the business survive? Is there still ice cream to be served?" Carmella asked, her voice filled with concern for Chad's parents.

He grinned. "It gave us a huge boost in sales that hasn't stopped since. You know what they say about bad publicity. There really is no such thing."

"Wow," was all I could muster up in response.

Not that I had hoped for the downfall of his family business or anything, but hearing how the videos had made it even more popular instead of the opposite was surreal, to say the least.

"Sorry that took so long." Raul suddenly appeared, as if out of thin air, holding so many plates that I wasn't sure where he'd put them all. Thankfully, he'd brought the bottle of wine over, and he refilled my and Carmella's glasses to the rim.

"Thank you," I said with a smile.

I planned on finishing my entire glass.

Raul squeezed as much of our food as he could onto our tabletop before pulling a standing serving tray to the side and leaving the rest of what we all ordered on it.

"We look like we haven't eaten in days," I said with a laugh as I reached for my pizza, which was so hot that steam was rising off of the pepperonis.

Everyone mumbled out unintelligible words before the talking stopped completely and our table grew deadly quiet. A mere two minutes ago, we couldn't shut up, and now, we couldn't stop eating.

FOR AS HUNGRY as I'd been, my stomach sure got full quickly. I glanced down and noticed that I'd only eaten two slices. Normally, I could put away four before my belly started aching and begged me to stop.

Oh well. More for breakfast, I thought to myself.

Or a late-night snack.

Or both.

"What are you grinning at?" River held me with his gaze, and I dropped the smile from my lips.

I hadn't even known I'd been doing it.

"Just daydreaming," I answered, the wine finally swimming in my veins, making me want to be a little bit nicer to my sworn enemy for once.

"About me? You really shouldn't." He winked, and the wine niceties ended.

"Never about you," I groaned. "And always about food. It's far more satisfying than you could ever be."

I felt good about my comeback, proud even. Until he leveled me with one of his own.

"It's not. Not like you'll ever know."

I flashed him a dirty look at took a drink of my wine instead of saying something in response.

"Why are you two like this?" Carmella interrupted our insults, waving a finger between me and River while she frowned at us. "Is it foreplay?"

"Carmella!" I shouted, almost spitting out my wine in the process.

"I think it's their names." Chad's voice was slow and slurred, and I whipped my head around to look at him.

"Our names?" I spit out, and Chad nodded, his eyes glassy.

"River. Sky. You're both elements. Or pieces of elements. I mean, don't you think it's weird that you two have names like that? It's like you were made for each other. You could have babies and name them Ocean and Star."

He started cracking up, like his suggestion was the funniest thing he'd ever heard. Apparently, it was because Carmella tried to stop from giggling, but couldn't.

"Ocean and Star. HA!" he said again, and they both laughed, each one holding their stomachs.

"Okay, Cookies and Cream, I think you've had enough," River said with a pat to Chad's back, and that actually made me snicker in response.

"Don't get pissed at me because you haven't landed her yet." Chad pointed at River, and I knew in that moment that they'd talked about me at some point before we checked into the hotel.

I had pretty much expected it, but it was still a little unnerving. Assuming something had been discussed versus it being confirmed that it had were two totally different things. River had talked about me to Chad. And told him that we never hooked up. Of course he had said that. It was the truth after all. River might be a man-whoring pig, but he didn't lie.

I guess the guy has one redeeming quality.

"You two act like you hate each other, but you don't. At all. You want to bone each other's brains out. But you keep lying about it. To yourselves. To everyone. But we all see it. The secret looks. The lust. Like Carmella said, it's all foreplay."

I rubbed at my temples, hoping that drunk Chad would stop talking. "You're severely delusional. The hatred is very real on my end."

"Not that anyone even knows why." River sounded annoyed and a little excited. Like he'd wanted the chance to talk about this, but never had the opportunity before.

I attempted to glare at River from across the table, but I was a little buzzed and wasn't entirely sure that my face was doing what I asked of it. I probably looked tired and uncomfortable instead.

"Why do you hate me? I've never even done a damn thing to you."

"I'm entitled to my opinion," I said before taking another drink of wine. If my mouth was full, I couldn't put my foot in it.

"Opinion based on what? You've hated me since the day we first worked together," he explained, like this was news to me, but I only nodded.

"Yep."

"Before I even opened my mouth and said two words to you, it was all dirty looks and huffs and bad body language," he continued, his mouth forming a snarl as he said the words.

Apparently, he didn't enjoy my initial reaction toward

him. I figured he never gave it a second thought after our shifts ended. I went to open my mouth and push his buttons even more, but Carmella beat me to the punch.

"One of us probably told her to." Carmella raised her hand in the air, and I watched as River focused on her. "I'm sure someone did."

"Told her to hate me?" he asked, sounding offended and baffled.

"Well, I mean, not hate you per se. But we do tell all the new girls to stay away from the pilots. And to definitely not date them."

"I thought that was just a rumor," Chad said, stumbling over the words.

"Nope." Carmella emphasized before adding, "But it's not like they listen, so it doesn't even matter."

River waved a hand in my direction. "She listened."

"Then, she's the only one," Carmella fired back.

"Can you two stop talking about me like I'm not here?" I said a little too loudly.

"Fine," River shouted back, his blue eyes piercing into mine. "Did someone tell you to stay away from me?" He leaned back in his chair and folded his arms across his chest.

"Yes."

"What about me?" Chad asked.

"No, not you, just pilots in general. Like, to stay away from them." I tried to play it off like it was no big deal, but neither Chad nor River seemed to be taking it that way.

Chad was disappointed that he hadn't been named, and River was angry that he had.

"So, someone told you to stay away from me *specifically*?" River pushed.

He was not going to let this go until I answered.

"They did."

"Who?" He actually sounded upset, and I didn't want to get Stacy in any kind of trouble with him or make work awkward for her.

"I really don't want to say."

"Sky," he growled.

"River," I tried to mimic, but I just sounded silly instead, and Carmella laughed.

"Don't ask her to rat out her friends," she said, trying to help the situation, but failing because River was pushy and relentless and used to getting what he wanted.

"Just trying to figure out who not to trust, is all."

Yep. He was pissed. And taking this way too far.

"It's really not a big deal. You're turning this into something it isn't. Can't we just let it go?"

He uncrossed his arms and made wild arm gestures while he spoke instead. "Sure. Fine. I'll let it go. For now," River huffed before finishing off his beer in one giant gulp.

He would definitely not be letting this go.

CALLING IT A NIGHT

SKY

W E EACH ORDERED one more drink, but I barely touched mine. I'd already had enough, and even after eating, my head was still swimming in an alcohol-induced pool. Chad was having trouble staying upright. He wobbled in his chair, clearly unbalanced and inebriated beyond a simple buzz.

"Do you need help getting up to your room?" River asked, but Chad shoved him away. Anytime River touched him, Chad swatted at his hand.

"Stop touching me. I don't need your help. I'll take hers though," Chad said, staring right at me with eyes that were half-closed. I wasn't even sure how he could see at this point.

"My help?" I stuttered, clearly shocked and a little scared.

I did not want to be the one to help Chad to his room.

"Come on, Sky, baby." Chad tried to sound charming, but he was wasted and getting sloppier by the second. "Take me to my room. I'll make it worth your while. Multiple times. I can get you ice cream."

Things were definitely starting to spiral, and I took it as my cue to go so I could finally take that bath I'd been dreaming about since we had first gotten here. I gestured toward Raul that I'd like to take my pizza to my room, and he gave me a nod in understanding before quickly disappearing. He couldn't come back with a box fast enough.

"Sky, come on. Stay with me tonight." Chad used both hands to push up from the table.

He took a stumbling step in my direction, but River was instantly there, blocking him from reaching me, like a wall made of muscle.

"Don't," River growled, his tone no longer joking or even friendly.

I'd never seen him so intense and focused. Whatever scene was happening in front of me, my body reacted to it like a live wire. I was instantly amped up and turned on. Protective River was sexy as hell, especially when I was the one he was defending. I'd never had a man stand up for me before. I wanted to jump on his back and ride him up to my room.

"She can speak for herself. Can't you, Sky? Come on, baby. Just one night. No one told you to stay away from me. They only told you to stay away from him. He's off-limits. I'm not."

Chad tried to shove River out of the way but failed. River was almost a foot taller and was definitely stronger. The only way he'd get past River and reach me was if River allowed it.

And that definitely wasn't happening.

River glanced over his shoulder, and his deep blue eyes looked almost pained, like he hated being put in this position. He was probably pissed that he was being forced to defend my honor.

"Touch Sky and you'll regret it. Do you hear me? Are you listening?" River was questioning Chad, who kept trying to get around him. "Leave her the fuck alone, or we're going to have a problem. Tell me you understand what I'm saying to you." River was making a mockery of the guy, treating him like a little child, but honestly, Chad deserved it.

"What if she wants me to touch her?" Chad asked, his words still slurring.

"She doesn't," River answered for me.

"She hates you. Not me," Chad continued to argue.

"She doesn't hate me," River snapped, and I huffed before being distracted by Raul.

He placed an empty to-go container in front of me, and I shoved my extra slices inside as quickly as I could.

"I'm going to head upstairs and call it a night," I announced, desperate to get away from this situation.

I couldn't leave the bar fast enough.

"I'll walk you up," River said forcefully.

It wasn't a request, and I did not have a say in the matter.

"Are you thinking what I'm thinking?" Chad was trying to whisper to Carmella, but he was loud and too drunk to have any real volume control.

"That we should all go to bed?" she asked, and he laughed, patting her forearm with his hand as he sat back down in his chair.

"You're funny," he said with a grin. "But no. Those two are going to hook up and then lie to our faces about it tomorrow. If she's not fucking me tonight, she's definitely fucking him."

My mouth dropped open, and my eyes instantly shot to River. I'd never seen him look so angry. His hands were balled into fists, and his jaw was clenched so tight that I thought I heard his teeth grinding. He was going to kill Chad. And I wasn't sure that I'd blame him for it.

"Chad, I'll politely ask you one time to shut your fucking mouth. I'm giving you a pass because you're hammered, but it's the only one you'll get. Talk about Sky again, and it will be the last thing you do for this airline."

"You can't do that," Chad huffed, his face turning even redder than before.

"I can. And I will," River threatened before taking a menacing step toward Chad. "I dare you to fucking test me."

River hovered, making sure that Chad didn't move a

muscle in my direction, before he added, "And you owe Sky an apology."

Before I could argue or say it wasn't necessary, Chad was stuttering, his words affected by the alcohol, his anger, and his embarrassment. He didn't want to give me anything, least of all an apology.

"I'm sorry, Sky," he said, his tone filled with anything but remorse.

He wasn't sorry. But I didn't care. I just wanted to get away from him. Chad's level of drunkenness and behavior was unacceptable from a professional standpoint. If I wanted to, I could report him to management and make sure we never crossed paths again. He could get in a lot of trouble. Not for the drinking, but for the harassment. Our airline took that stuff very seriously.

"Let's go." River grabbed me by the arm and started to lead me away.

I shook out of his grip. "You don't need to manhandle me." I balanced the pizza in my other hand, trying not to drop it.

"Sorry," he grumbled, and I could tell that he wasn't even remotely okay with everything that had just occurred.

He pressed the elevator button before facing me, his expression pained. "Did I hurt you?"

"No. I just …" So many thoughts were crashing together in my head, and even though I'd always hated River, the very last thing I was feeling right now was animosity. I was grateful he had been there.

The doors opened, and we stepped inside.

"Thank you for standing up for me."

I watched as he pressed the button for the seventh floor, and my mind started imagining what else his fingers could do. They could touch my body, explore my curves, get tangled in my hair, plunge inside me, make me come.

"It was the right thing to do," he said, almost nonchalant, like he would have done it for anyone and I wasn't special. Maybe he would have. Maybe I wasn't.

When the elevator dinged for our floor, he held the doors with one hand while I exited first. I stopped abruptly, and River almost ran into my back before I turned to face him. Without warning, I threw my free arm around his waist and buried my face in his chest. I was hugging River.

His strong body melted against mine as he bent down

to cover me in a protective stance. I swore I heard him groan and not out of displeasure either. He liked touching me.

"You know, they also called him Half-Pint Chad," I said with a smirk as I pushed away from him and tried to break the awkward scenario I'd just created by touching him so intimately.

"Because he's short?"

"I think it was both. A dig at his height and the ice cream thing."

River laughed as I finally started heading toward our rooms … which were next to each other … with an adjoining door between them. If I opened mine and he opened his …

Ugh! I admonished myself for even thinking those thoughts, so I tried to push them away. *The guy did one nice, sexy, super-hot thing, and you throw your hatred out the window along with your pants? Think about Stacy and how much he hurt her.*

Was River worth losing a girlfriend over?

Was any guy?

When I reached my door, River stood dangerously

close to me, both of us holding our key cards in our hands, but neither one of us racing to get inside, like we had before. I could feel the heat penetrating from his body. I was supposed to hate him, but the feeling was eluding me. My hard shell toward him had cracked and was chipping away.

"Sky?" His voice hung in the air between us like a cloud.

"Uh-huh?" I mumbled in response, unsure of what he might say next.

"Maybe tomorrow, you can tell me who made you hate me so much."

I blew out a soft laugh. "Well, I hate you a little less right now, if that counts for anything."

He tried to close the gap between us, but I stepped back until I was pressed against the door. His arms encircled my body, holding me in place, and I couldn't stop staring at his mouth.

Was he going to kiss me? Did I want him to?

Don't do it.

Please do it.

Oh God.

"Well, I don't hate you right now at all. I might even …" He paused, and I wanted to scream at him to finish the thought.

"Might even what?"

He shook his head, clearly content with driving me out of my mind. "Nah. It doesn't matter."

"I'm definitely starting to hate you again," I said because I didn't enjoy not getting my way.

He leaned down close to me, his lips brushing against my ear, and I swore my knees almost buckled on the spot. I held my breath as he spoke. "I know how to make you stop. Just tell me, Sky. Who said it?"

"I can't," I said, hoping my words weren't as shaky as my body currently was.

"You can. It's easy. Just tell me."

"I can't." I swallowed hard, my resolve crumbling for no good reason other than his nearness.

I waffled between keeping the information to myself and giving him what he wanted. His thumb was under my chin, gently lifting my face so I could focus on those blue eyes that I suddenly didn't find myself despising.

"Who did I upset, Sky?" He asked the question so

softly that I couldn't help but respond.

The name slipped out from under my tongue.

"Stacy."

"Who the hell is Stacy?" His eyes pulled together as he shook his head and took a step away from my body, leaving me cold and empty.

I almost believed that he didn't know who I was talking about. But that proved my point as to the kind of guy he was.

"Oh my God. See? This is why I have to hate you. Good night, River."

HIT THE DAMN GYM

RIVER

"*T*HIS IS WHY *I have to hate you. Good night, River.*"

I was a fucked-up bag of mixed emotions as I paced inside my hotel room, knowing that Sky was just a wall away. That damn door between us taunted me with every step I took. I could break it down if I wanted to. Rip it off the fucking hinges and kick at it until there was nothing but splintered wood and sawdust.

Dropping to the bed, I put my head between my knees and tried to focus on calming down. But there were too many things happening at once in my head.

Who the hell is Stacy? And what did she say to Sky that made her hate me without even knowing me?

I still couldn't place the woman. I knew that made me sound like an asshole, but it was the truth. *Stacy who?* It was driving me crazy.

And then there was Chad. I was still pissed at all the things he'd said to Sky tonight. He had been out of line, unprofessional, and lucky I didn't break his jaw just to get him to shut up. The worst part was that through all of the sexual propositions he'd made, it had forced me to realize something I hadn't expected.

If anyone was going to be fucking Sky, it was going to be me.

The idea of her and him together made me feel things I wasn't used to and didn't necessarily like. I was not the jealous type. *At all.* But imagining another man's hands touching her skin was enough to make me seethe with it. I was used to being on the winning side of things, and with Sky, I was constantly losing.

I didn't want to lose when it came to her anymore.

Realizing that I wanted her opened up a whole other set of complications. I'd sworn off coworkers. Decided to stop hooking up with them for the betterment of my career, but there was something about the fiery redhead in the room next door that made me want to throw all my self-control out the window and fuck her until we were nothing but a tangled mess of sweaty and exhausted limbs.

Sky wanted it too. I had seen it in her eyes. Her hatred for me had been replaced with something else entirely. I had seen the way she stared at my mouth, wondering what I was going to do with it. She'd wanted me to kiss her just as badly as I'd wanted to do it. And she wouldn't have stopped me once I started either. Which was a good thing because I was certain that once I got a taste of that woman, I'd never want to quit.

My dick started throbbing, and it only made me more frustrated. There was no way I'd be able to sleep anytime soon even if I went and jacked off to mental images of Sky in the shower. I was too worked up. Too deep in my own head.

Grabbing my duffel bag, I searched through it and quickly changed into my gym clothes and Adidas.

This was nothing a good workout couldn't fix.

PUNISHING MYSELF WITH cardio and heavy weights didn't

quite help the way I'd thought it would. I should have known better. I'd never been able to outrun my mind ... but it'd never stopped me from trying.

All my thoughts did were grow stronger and more intense with each set. My dick even got hard. *AT THE GYM!* I couldn't get Sky's face out of my head. The look in her eyes, her full ruby-red lips. I wanted all of it. Thoughts of her were consuming me like a drug. The more I tried to push her away, the more forceful she became.

Fuck it, I said out loud as I dropped the dumbbells to the floor with a thud.

There was only one way to deal with this.

I took the elevator upstairs and knocked on her door. My body was covered in sweat, but I didn't care how I looked or smelled. Her door flew open, her body wrapped in only a towel. When she realized that it was me standing there, she reached across her breasts, holding the flimsy white fabric in place.

"I have to do this," I said as I reached for her.

My mouth covered hers before she could speak or question what I was doing. She tasted like pizza and wine and toothpaste. My tongue snaked inside, dancing with hers, while I held her tight against me. Her body arched into my grasp before I felt her tense up. I broke the kiss even though I didn't want to.

"I was going to die if I didn't get the chance to do that," I admitted before noticing the horrified look on her face. "I know I'm not that bad of a kisser."

"You're definitely not." She tried to hide her grin, still holding on to her towel with both hands. "But I can't do this with you, River."

"Because you hate me?" I asked, knowing that she damn well didn't. Not anymore. Not after tonight.

"No. Because Stacy still likes you."

"I'm not trying to be a dick here, but I really don't know who you're talking about." I pressed a hand against the doorframe and leaned against it.

She propped her hip to the side, stretching the towel to its limit. "Are you messing with me?"

"I'm not. What did she tell you I did to her? I really don't know."

I was being dead serious, and I wasn't sure if that made Sky question my character even more or if she wanted to give me the benefit of the doubt, but she let out an exasperated groan.

"Come inside," she directed before turning her back to me. "Let me get dressed."

I wanted to argue and tell her no. That she should sit next to me in nothing but a towel so I could do all the things I'd been daydreaming about doing to her for the last hour. But I didn't.

It was crazy how quickly emotions could flip. One second, I'd thought she was a stuck-up snob, and the next, I wanted to bury myself so deep inside her that she'd feel me for weeks.

When she stepped out of the bathroom, she was in a tank top and baggy sweatpants. Neither of those items did anything to turn me off. There was a chaise lounge in her room, and I moved to sit there instead of the bed. It seemed like the safer option if I wanted to stay focused on the subject matter and not stare at her tits all night.

Sky sat on the bed and crossed her legs, staring at me. I wasn't sure if she was waiting for me to initiate the conversation, but I took it as my cue to say at least something on the matter.

"So, Stacy," I said, dragging out her name like it was

unfamiliar and I'd never said it before.

"Don't say her name like that." Sky tried not to laugh, but it slipped out anyway.

"Sorry. So, what did she say?"

I'd never cared what the flight attendants said about me before, but now, I was more than curious. Whatever had been told to Sky was enough to make her treat me like shit from day one and never give me a chance to get to know her. We had gone straight from being introduced to enemies.

"She said you guys dated, and then you basically ghosted her."

"She said I Ice Cream Chad'd her?" I asked, horrified at the comparison I'd just done to myself.

"I guess, yeah." Sky was grinning, and then her face looked like she had bitten into something sour. "Ew. Please don't compare yourself to him again. He's foul."

I was grateful that she didn't think we deserved to be in the same category. That was definitely a win for me. "He is, right? Kind of a jerk?"

Her eyes swung to mine. "Kind of? He's abhorrent."

"But I'm not?" I questioned, forcing her to say out

loud that I wasn't, for both my benefit and hers.

"I'm not sure yet." She smirked.

Still a win.

"Anyway, back to Stacy and this whole *we dated, and I stopped talking to her* thing. I didn't do that. I *don't* do that. I haven't dated anyone in a long time."

I'd hooked up with women in the past, but I wasn't a dick about it. And I'd never *dated* anyone from work. I hadn't had a real girlfriend since high school.

Sky looked around the room, her eyes bouncing from the floor to the ceiling. "Maybe you slept together and then never talked to her again?"

"I know you're not going to believe me, but I don't do that. I don't fuck women and never speak to them again."

She started coughing. "Why not? That seems like a very River Santos thing to do."

"How would you know?" I asked, my tone bordering on rude, but her assumptions were agitating, and I was tired of this game.

Her lips pressed, forming a straight line. "No. You're right. I wouldn't."

"You do realize that you've hated me this whole time

because of something one person said to you that might or might not even be true."

I was finally calling her out and clearing the air. I wanted to get to the bottom of this so we could pack it up and put it behind us for good.

"I'm starting to realize that, but still ..." She looked almost embarrassed, like she might not finish her thought.

"But still what?" I pressed, urging her to continue.

"You just seemed to fit the profile. The way you act. The way you look." She waved her hand toward me. "Stacy said you leave a trail of broken hearts across the airline, and when I heard the other stories about you, I just believed them all."

"You ladies are really gossipy," was all I could muster up as a response without getting into specifics of my sexual history.

"We are. Plus, it's not like you were ever nice to me, so hating you was easy."

I let out a loud, warring sound. "Me? You were rude from the start. I only reacted in kind."

She gave me a soft look. "Yeah, I can see that."

"So, you admit that you started this." I grinned, and her

lips tilted up.

"Maybe."

"I want to finish it," I said, and her jovial expression instantly dropped into something far more serious.

"Finish what?" She sounded so nervous.

"All of this. Whatever this shit is between us. I want it dead and buried so we can move past it."

"Move past it to what exactly?"

I was scaring her. Coming on way too strong and way too fast. She'd spent the last three years hating my guts and thinking that I was a typical guy who didn't give a shit about women or their feelings. I couldn't blame her for feeling a little jarred by my relationship whiplash. We'd gone from trading barbs in the bar earlier to me shoving my tongue down her throat and telling her I wanted more.

But I did want more. That much had become blatantly apparent. And now that I'd realized it, I couldn't get the desire out of my head. I wasn't the type of man who gave up easily once he set his mind to something.

"Do you have a picture of Stacy?"

"I do," she said before lunging for her phone, which was charging on the nightstand next to her bed. I watched her scroll through what I assumed was her gallery in search of one. "Here. She's all the way on the left. Dark hair."

I grabbed the device and enlarged the photo so I could see it better. The memory came crashing back in that instant.

"You remember, don't you?" Sky asked as I handed her cell back to her. She sounded sort of disappointed, like she had wanted this all to be a misunderstanding of some kind.

"Yeah. Stacy. I haven't seen her in a long time. I forgot all about her. But it's not what you think," I said, and Sky straightened her legs in front of her.

"You didn't hook up with her?"

"I mean, we kissed, but that's it."

"That's it?"

"Yeah," I said, remembering everything about that night now that I'd seen Stacy's face.

"So, you didn't sleep with her?" Sky was trying to make it all make sense.

"No. She was really drunk."

Sky's eyes narrowed. "Maybe she doesn't remember.

Maybe she thinks you guys did something you didn't, and that's why she's so hurt over it."

"It's possible." I leaned forward, putting my elbows on my knees. "But I promise you, Sky, we didn't sleep together. She was way too drunk for that. I did walk her to her room and put her in her bed. But I didn't stay there with her. I left right after I made sure she was safe."

Her green eyes held on to mine as she delivered three words I never thought I'd hear her say. "I believe you."

"You do?"

She nodded. "Yeah. For whatever reason, River, I don't think that you're a liar."

"Thanks?"

"I know that didn't sound like a compliment, but it was. Hating you has been exhausting. But it's also been kind of fun. You're always quick with the comebacks, which I appreciate. Keeps me on my toes."

I stopped myself from laughing. "I want to disagree with you, but whenever we fly together, it's as infuriating as it is exciting. I never know what you'll say next. It pisses me off, but a part of me enjoys it."

I pushed to a stand and pulled her curtains back to look

outside. The snow was falling so heavily that I couldn't see anything, except for a solid blanket of white. We were definitely going to be stuck in this hotel for the foreseeable future.

"I am sorry though. For being so mean all the time. I know I take it too far sometimes."

"I accept your apology. And I'm sorry too. About earlier." I let the fabric go and turned to face her right as she took a step closer to me. I hadn't even heard her get up from the bed and move in my direction.

"For which part?" She was looking up at me, her eyelashes batting, tempting me to take her in my arms and worship every inch of her.

I grabbed one of her hands and brought it to my lips, pressing a gentle kiss there. "For what I said about your dad. I obviously didn't know."

The hand I was holding tensed, and instead of dropping it, I held on tighter.

"Thank you. I appreciate you saying that."

"Were you two close?" I asked, knowing that I was opening myself up to the same line of questioning from her. I was willing to go there.

"We were." She pulled her hand from mine, but didn't step away. "The holidays hurt so much without him. It's not the same, you know?"

"I can imagine," I said because I didn't know what it was like to lose a parent to death. Both of mine were still alive. Even though I had little to no respect for my father anymore, he was still breathing and around whenever I visited.

"Are your parents still married?" she asked, and I gave her a curt nod.

"If you can call it that," I said, and she looked sad for me.

"What does that mean?"

"It means that my dad was a habitual cheater, and my mom felt stuck since she didn't have a job, so she stayed with him instead of leaving."

Sky sucked in a long, deep breath before blowing it out slowly, digesting everything I'd just said. "And that's why you don't lie."

"Huh?"

I'd never put the two things together before, but she was probably right. I hated the way my father constantly lied, even after getting caught. I never understood why he didn't just own up to his indiscretions, but maybe it was because he wasn't sorry for them. Admitting that he'd had multiple affairs should have been followed by an apology, and that was something he didn't want to give.

I wasn't sure I'd ever heard my father apologize in my entire life now that I thought about it.

"When you grow up with someone who lies a lot, you go one of two ways. You either adopt that behavior because it's familiar. Or you despise it so much that you become the polar opposite. I think you took the opposite route."

"I think you might be onto something," I agreed because she was right.

That was exactly what I'd done. I didn't want to be anything like my father, so I'd made sure that I wasn't. Not in that regard anyway.

"Were you supposed to go home for Thanksgiving?" I asked, redirecting the conversation a little. Not because I was uncomfortable, but because there wasn't anything else to say really. Those few sentences had told Sky more about my personality and upbringing than an hour's worth of conversation could have.

She nodded. "Yeah. My mom's going to read me the riot act when she gets my message in the morning."

"It's not like you control the weather," I said, pulling back the curtain once more as she moved to the side of me and looked outside.

"No, but I took this job, knowing that I'd be gone all the time. I'm not sure she's forgiven me for that."

"But you love it, right? The job?" I wondered if she enjoyed her side of the business as much as I did.

The way her face lit up told me everything I needed to know.

"I do. There are so many perks and so few drawbacks. The irritations are minor in comparison to everything else."

I wrapped my arm around her middle and pulled her body against me. She was stiff as a board before quickly melting into my side like we'd done this a thousand times before. It didn't escape me how well we fit together, like two halves of the same mold. Glancing down, I pressed a kiss to the top of her head, and she looked up at me, her lips begging for my attention.

"I'm going to kiss you," I warned before leaning down and doing exactly that.

I DID SOMETHING BAD

SKY

HOW HAD WE gotten to this point? River's tongue was in my mouth, and I was currently drowning in ecstasy, like I'd been wanting this my whole life. His hands moved all over my body, refusing to stay in one place for too long. Everywhere he touched lit a fire inside of me and a trail of warmth on my skin.

I'd spent so much time hating this guy, thinking that he was nothing more than a typical player who didn't care about who he hurt in the process, and I'd been wrong. About so many things.

Wrong about him and Stacy ... about him not having a soul ... or a heart ... or feelings. River had all of those things. And they were beautiful. After the way that he'd defended me earlier tonight, I felt like a goner for the guy. If Chad had pushed him just a little further, River would have snapped on my behalf.

Maybe I shouldn't find that kind of thing sexy, but I did.

When we finally broke the kiss, we were breathless and flustered. I could tell that we both wanted to take things further physically, but mentally, we were each warring inside. The night had done a complete one-eighty, and I needed a little time to get my bearings.

Even though I believed what River had said about Stacy and the night that never was, I still felt obligated to talk to her before he and I went any further.

Whatever was happening between River and me didn't feel like a superficial fling.

It felt like the start of something more. And it was happening at warp speed.

"I don't do one-night stands," I blurted out before I could stop my mouth from saying the words.

River rolled his eyes at me, making sure I saw the gesture. "That's not what I want."

"What do you want then?"

"More than one night—that's for sure."

"I don't do casual sex. It's either all or nothing for me, Pilot Santos."

If my words scared him, he didn't show it. But he needed to know the truth. I wasn't the kind of woman who gave her vagina away on a whim. My heart was attached to it. They were a package deal. You couldn't have one without the other.

"I know that," he said, and there was no possible way for him to know anything that personal about me. I was tempted to argue, to ask him a hundred questions in rebuttal, but I didn't have to. "I stalk your social media sometimes. I figured you out a long time ago."

"You think you know everything," I countered, and he grinned.

"You just hate that I do."

"Go to your own room." I pointed at the door, and his lips brushed against my neck before reaching my ear.

"I will, but only for tonight. Enjoy sleeping alone, Sky. It's your last night doing it."

My mouth fell open with his words, and I watched him

walk to the adjoining door, unlock my side, and disappear through it. At some point, he'd opened his. I had no idea when, and I definitely hadn't heard him do it.

I speed-walked to the one on my side and closed it, but didn't set the lock. If he tried, he'd figure out that he could get through it.

I needed to think about what I'd just done and the line that I'd crossed.

Neither one of us was going to take what had just happened back. If anything, we were going to move forward.

River wasn't the villain I'd always believed him to be.

How the hell was I going to tell Stacy without her hating me for it?

I WOKE UP and immediately remembered what I'd done with River. Burying my head in my pillow, I felt myself grinning, the excitement blossoming inside of me before I shut it down, a pit forming in my stomach instead.

Stacy still had feelings for River.

And I had not only let him kiss me, but I'd kissed him back.

Did that make me a bad friend?

Probably.

No, it definitely did.

Grabbing the covers and holding them tight, I blew out a breath, trying to figure out exactly what to do. Maybe I'd ask Carmella for advice. She was older and generally wiser even though she hadn't exactly been helpful in the bar last night, egging Chad on with her nonstop laughter.

Ugh. Speaking of Chad, he'd ruined everything.

I wasn't sure how I'd handle seeing him today or how I'd feel when I did. What if he wasn't sorry or tried to hit on me all over again? River wouldn't be so forgiving if that happened. I hated being uncomfortable, especially since we were all stuck here together until the storm let up.

Reaching for my phone, I noticed the text message and missed call from my mom. She told me to call her as soon as I woke up. I groaned out loud, knowing that I needed to mentally prepare myself for the sound of her disappointment. I wasn't awake enough to deal with it quite yet. Maybe after I ate some cold pizza.

Someone knocked on my door three times.

"Hold on," I shouted as I threw the covers off and

padded down the hall, rubbing my eyes.

Checking my reflection in the mirror, I prayed that it wasn't River. I looked awful, and I didn't really want him to see me like this. Glancing in the peephole, I saw the last person I'd expected to see. My heart dropped to my stomach as I pulled the door open and faked a smile.

"Stacy?" I asked.

She squealed and threw her arms around me before pushing her way inside. I followed behind her tiny body, watching as she made herself comfortable on my bed.

"What are you doing here?" I asked, sounding like a bit of a jerk, but not meaning to.

I was just surprised.

"We got in late last night."

"I thought the hotel was sold out?"

"They found us one room. One room for four of us, Sky. I haven't slept at all."

She sounded dramatic as she reached for a pillow and propped it up behind her head, a groan slipping from her lips.

"How'd you find my room?"

"I saw Carmella on her way out," she said as her eyes

started to close. "She told me which one was yours."

"Wait. Carmella was leaving?" I ran to the window, threw open the curtain, and looked outside. It was still snowing. Hard.

"Yeah. She was going to the train station with that one first officer guy. The short one."

"Chad," I said.

She nodded, her eyes reopening. "Yeah."

"That means there're two rooms available if they checked out."

"They didn't check out, but I'm already ahead of you, sister." She flashed a key card at me.

I assumed she'd taken Carmella's room instead of Chad's, but only because it was what I would have done and not really any other reason.

"What if they come back? If the trains can't run?"

"Then, I'll stay with you," she said simply, like I was an idiot for even asking.

"Of course," I agreed as I pushed the selfish thoughts of not being able to spend more time alone with River out of my head.

There was a loud knock, and my heart started pounding like a drum. I knew who was behind that knock, but Stacy didn't.

"Who could that be?" she asked as she hopped up from the bed and ran to the front door, pulling it open like she expected Santa Claus himself to be behind it. "That's weird. There's no one here."

Another knock filled the air before the door in the center of the room pushed open and River stepped through it, holding food in a bag and a grin on his perfect face.

God, he was stunning.

"I brought you breakfast in." The words died on his tongue when he caught sight of Stacy standing there, staring at him like he had twelve heads.

"River? Why are you bringing Sky food? Why do you two have adjoining rooms? What the hell is going on?" Her head swiveled back and forth between us, her eyes narrowing as she tried to put the pieces together.

All at once, something must have clicked because she looked so hurt. So betrayed. And I couldn't even blame her. I hadn't had a chance to tell her about yesterday or what I'd done behind her back yet. She'd only been in my room for about five minutes.

"Did you two …" She pointed a finger before gasping. "Sky, you didn't. You wouldn't. You *hate* him." She emphasized the word.

"I know," I said. "I do," I agreed, and River made a hurt sound of his own. My eyes crashed into his, and I saw the sadness there. "I mean, I did. I don't"—I paused—"hate him anymore."

This was not going well, and I definitely wasn't making it any better with all my hesitation and stumbling.

"You don't hate him anymore?" She repeated my words, throwing them like knives back in my direction. "And why's that, Sky? There's only one way you'd stop hating him," she said, and I dreaded what was coming next. "And that's if you fucked him."

The fact that I stood there with my mouth open, not saying a word, didn't help my cause. I was too stunned to speak. Too caught off guard to form a sentence that wouldn't sound like a toddler babbling and make me seem even guiltier than I already was.

"You've got to be kidding me." She sounded so repulsed as she shook her head slowly, her anger coming off of her in waves. I could *feel* it. "Enjoy your Thanksgiving together. I hope you choke on your turkey," she said before storming out of my room and slamming the door so hard that I thought the pictures might fall off the walls.

I looked at River, my shock still palpable as he put the paper bag that he was holding on top of the dresser next to the TV. He stepped in front of my body and reached for my shoulders with both hands, forcing me to make eye contact with him. Then, he pressed a kiss to my lips. I wasn't even sure I moved or puckered my lips to kiss him back.

"I got this, babe. I'll be right back."

HAPPY THANKSGIVING TO US

RIVER

I LEFT SKY standing there like a statue as I hauled ass out the door, chasing after one pissed off and hurt flight attendant. I had known the two of them were friends—Sky had told me that—but seeing how devastated she had looked after Stacy said those things to her really made it all hit home.

They weren't just coworkers and casual acquaintances, like I was with my fellow pilots. Someone you worked with and then never talked to again until you crossed paths once more. No. Stacy and Sky cared about each other and probably spoke or texted every day, the way real friends did.

It tore me up to watch Sky take all the blame for what had happened between us. I was, after all, the real reason why Stacy was angry in the first place. I felt obligated to fix things and fill in the blanks for her where I knew she must have some.

"Stacy, stop," I shouted as I caught up to her in the hallway and reached for her shoulder.

She swung around, tears in the corners of her eyes. "What do you want, River? Just go back to Sky."

"No. I want to talk to you," I said, and she shook her head. "About that night."

"Oh, so now, you want to talk about that night?"

"It's not what you think. Can we talk? Please?" I wasn't above begging.

I hated that Stacy thought whatever she did about the two of us when it wasn't even remotely close to the truth. And she'd been holding on to false memories for years. *Years.* And I'd had no idea this entire time. I was the only one who could clear it all up.

"Come on," she begrudgingly agreed before opening the door to her room and walking inside.

I followed her in, keeping my distance as I glanced

around quickly. It was identical to Sky's, everything in the same place and positioning, and I sat down on the chaise lounge, like I'd done last night. Leaning forward, I put my elbows on my knees and waited for Stacy to get comfortable. She looked exhausted, but I wasn't about to tell her that.

"What do you want to talk about? How you got what you wanted and never talked to me again? How you hurt my feelings, but didn't care? How I fell for you and you made me feel stupid for doing it?"

Well, I guess we're jumping right in.

"Sure. But that's not what happened," I said, my tone serious and steady.

I refused to take the blame for something I hadn't done. I was man enough to take responsibility for my actions, but I wouldn't be taking them for something that never happened in the first place.

"What are you talking about? What are you trying to say?" She sounded more annoyed than anything else.

"Sky told me that you think we slept together."

"We did sleep together." Her eyes grew wide in an attempt to emphasize her point.

"No, Stacy. We didn't."

I watched as she bit her bottom lip before she started shaking her head, disagreeing with me.

"We did. I remember you in my room. And I remember you leaving."

"Which happened about three minutes apart," I said, my tone a little ruder than I'd meant, but it sent the point home.

"That's not right." Her forehead furrowed, creases forming with her confusion. "I remember," she insisted.

"You were really drunk," I explained. "I walked you to your room. I made sure you got into bed, and then I left you there."

"Seriously?"

The truth had to be sinking in by this point, but I could tell that she didn't want to accept it. She'd believed for so long now that we'd had sex, and now, here I was, telling her that we hadn't.

"I wouldn't lie to you about this. If we'd slept together, I'd tell you. But we didn't. And I took you to your room to make sure you didn't sleep with anyone else. You were way too drunk to give consent, and there're a lot of not-cool guys out there."

"Shit," she breathed out, and I knew in that moment that I'd finally gotten through to her. "This whole time …" She stopped before finishing her sentence, but I already knew what she was going to say. She didn't need to say it.

"I know."

"I told Sky to stay away from you. I told her it was because I still had feelings for you, but it was because I was mad at you and all the guys like you. I felt stupid more than anything else."

"So, you don't have feelings for me?" I teased, and she gave me a small grin.

"No. I thought you were a jerk, so I told her you were a player who sleeps with any willing woman who lets you and that she should stay away."

"Well, she listened to you for three years," I said with a laugh. "But I've got to tell you …"

"What?"

"I really like her. And I don't want that to be a problem between you two."

She folded her hands in her lap and blew out a long breath. "You're serious?"

"I am."

"I've never seen this side of you, River. It's sort of sweet."

I sensed a tinge of jealousy lingering in the background of her compliment.

"I want a shot with her, but she'll never give it to me if her being with me ruins your friendship. You have to forgive her. She didn't do anything wrong."

I was adamant about this. If Stacy punished Sky, there would always be this negative moment lingering between us. Sky would always think that her friendship ended because our relationship started. It was fucked up, and I didn't want that.

"Don't worry about me and Sky. We're fine. Promise." She pushed off the bed and stretched her arms over her head. "I can't believe we never slept together."

"I can't believe you thought that this whole time and I never even knew."

That was the craziest part of this whole thing in my opinion. Stacy had genuinely believed in something that had never happened, and I'd been in the dark about it the entire time even though I was the subject of it. It was truly enlightening what could go on in people's minds when you removed the communication aspect.

She reached for her phone and held it up. "I'll send Sky a text right now, telling her that I love her and that I give my blessing for your union."

"Maybe take back the whole 'choke on a turkey' thing?" I used air quotes around the words as soon as I remembered her saying them.

Stacy laughed. "Will do. I need a nap. Will you guys wake me up for dinner? I don't want to be alone on Thanksgiving. That's depressing."

"Of course. So, we're good? Everything's good?"

"We're good. Go get your girl. And don't screw it up," she warned as I headed toward her door.

I couldn't get back to Sky fast enough.

I DIDN'T KNOW why, but I went into my room and walked through our adjoining doors instead of knocking on her front door like a normal person.

"River?" Sky's voice lacked the timidness that it'd had earlier when Stacy was here.

The shock had apparently worn off, and while I'd been gone, Sky had gathered her bearings. And gotten dressed. Which was a damn shame because I planned on taking off all the clothes she'd just put on.

"Hey." She threw herself into my arms, and I held on tight, placing kisses on the top of her head like she belonged to me.

Because she did.

And she was about to realize exactly that.

"I assume it went well?" she asked before pulling out of my grasp.

"Did she text you?" I wondered because Stacy had told me she would, but I hadn't stuck around to make sure it actually happened.

"She did." Sky pursed her lips and tried to stop from smiling but failed.

It made me curious, so I asked, "Can you tell me what she said? You don't have to."

"She gave me her blessing and told me to choke on your dick instead of a turkey."

"Oh. Well, that can be arranged." I had to stop myself from unzipping my jeans and letting her have her way with me right then and there.

"Did she believe you?" Sky wanted the details of what had happened. Everything else could wait.

I filled her in, trying not to leave a single thing out. My mother had taught me that women asked a lot of questions because they wanted all the information. When men summed things up in one or two sentences, women often felt unsatisfied. I didn't want Sky to feel that way in any capacity.

"It seems too easy," she said once I finished telling her everything.

I'd had a feeling she'd react that way. Three years of built-up frustration and anger, wiped out in a single five-minute conversation? It felt like a trap.

"She's really not mad? And she's okay with this?" Sky wagged a finger between our two bodies.

"You read her text," I said, as if that alone was explanation enough.

If Stacy hadn't been okay, she wouldn't have sent those words—or made that brilliant suggestion.

"Speaking of that …" She grinned before dropping to her knees, and I swore I almost cried out with joy.

Her hands reached for the button on my jeans before sliding it through the hole. I stared down, watching her fingers move like this was too good to be true and might end at any second. The zipper was next, and I reveled in the sound of it being pulled down. Sky gripped the waistband of my jeans with both hands and lowered them from my body. I swore my dick almost hit her in the forehead. He was dying to be set free, and I wasn't going to stop her from doing it.

Free Willy, I thought to myself.

And she did.

Glancing up at me with lust-filled eyes, she licked her lips and refocused her attention on the task at hand. Before I could even think another thought, my dick was in her mouth. I swore I almost lost my balance from the feel of her wet tongue and hot breath surrounding me. She sucked and moaned, moving slow at first before she sped up her pace. My eyes rolled to the back of my head as I fumbled for something to hold on to. My hand thankfully found the top of the dresser, and I gripped the edge to stop from falling over.

My other hand tangled in the locks of her hair, settling

on the back of her head. I did my best not to push her, but the urge was overwhelming at times. I couldn't believe this was happening, and I didn't want to come in her mouth. Not yet.

Moving my hips away from her swollen lips, I removed myself from her mouth with a popping sound.

She looked up at me quickly, her face concerned. "Was it not okay?" she asked as I reached for her hands and helped her to her feet.

"It was too good. I had to stop."

She grinned at that.

"My turn," I warned before pointing at the bed.

Sky started to turn around and move in that direction, but I stopped her, spinning her back to face me. I kissed her hard, my tongue in her mouth, exploring every inch like I wanted to memorize the way it felt. Touching her lit a fire in my whole body, waking me up from whatever self-imposed slumber I'd been in. In all my years, I'd never felt like this.

I distracted her with kisses while I undressed her. I honestly wasn't sure she even realized it was happening until I felt her body shiver underneath my touch. Each place her naked skin pressed against mine, warmth spread. She was so soft. I couldn't wait to find out what she tasted like, so I dropped to my knees and started kissing her thigh. Her hands instantly gripped my shoulders, her fingernails digging in. I kind of liked the pain, so I didn't make a sound, and I definitely didn't stop.

When my tongue swept across her, I wasn't sure who moaned louder—her or me. She liked the way it felt, and I wanted to drown in her flavor. Reaching for her ass, I lifted her up and onto the bed before spreading her legs even wider.

Let the Thanksgiving feast begin. Who needs anything else to eat when I have this?

When she finally fell apart, it was beautiful. Her entire body shuddered in the aftermath as I crawled on top of her, hovering, my dick already covered in a condom I'd fished out of my jeans pocket.

"Condom," she said, her voice breathless and heady.

"Already on."

"Thank God."

Her hands skated down my back, one inching its way toward my hardness. When she grabbed the tip and started guiding it toward her entrance, I thought I might come right there in her hand. I felt fifteen again before I pulled it the fuck together. Pushing inside, I fought the urge to start hammering her into the headboard as hard and as fast as I could. She was tight, but so damn wet and slippery.

I moved painfully slow, pushing in as deep as I could go before pulling back out and doing it all again. Her back arched with my movements, allowing me to hit even deeper. It felt like I was going over a cliff each time I plunged into her. It wasn't long before everything started to overwhelm me in the best possible way. But I wasn't going to last.

I leaned lower so I could claim her mouth, and we shared the same air as I stared at her, watching the way her eyes opened and closed without warning. Her hips kept grinding up into me, and I knew I was close.

"I'm going to come, babe."

"Please do," she moaned, her hips still grinding and circling against me.

I started thrusting faster. Harder. I couldn't get enough. The pressure built up inside me, and I spilled into the condom covering me. When I opened my eyes, Sky was watching me, a ghost of a smile on her lips.

I leaned down to kiss her before easing out and lying down next to her warm body.

She propped herself up on one arm and ran a hand down my chest before pressing a kiss there. "When can we do it again?"

THANKFUL

SKY

RIVER AND I had sex three more times before we even attempted to get dressed and leave our hotel room. By that point, I was starving, and all the leftover pizza was long gone.

"I need food," I complained.

"That's why we're going downstairs," he said as he fixed his hair to perfection. Of course.

There was a knock on my door, and I hesitated for a second before pulling it open. Stacy stood there with her arms folded across her chest, a concerned look on her face. I noticed her carry-on bag next to her.

"Carmella and Chad are back. The trains were canceled."

The storm. I figured it was still raging outside, but I'd been too distracted to even think about it. Or care, to be honest.

"So, they need their rooms back?" I asked, already knowing the answer.

"You can have mine." River appeared at my side, holding out a key card toward Stacy.

"You sure?"

"Trust me. Between our two rooms, this is not the one you want," he said, and I watched as she surveyed the space, noting the discarded pieces of clothing lying haphazardly all over the place.

She wrinkled her nose. "River's room it is! Thanks."

"Let me get my stuff out," he said before disappearing through the adjoining door.

Stacy pushed her way inside. "It smells like sex in here."

I wasn't sure what to say, so I said nothing. What if she wasn't okay with my dating River now that it was in her face?

"You're not mad, right?" I decided to ask.

Her face quickly morphed into an apologetic expression as her head shook. "No. Not at all. I'm sorry I told you he was a bad person."

I shrugged. "It's okay. I mean, he is a pilot. And he did come off like a dick," I said with a light giggle.

"And now, he's your dick," she said, and my laughter grew louder.

Her words swam in my head before settling there. River, this man I'd hated for so long, was suddenly something else entirely. He was no longer my enemy. And I could picture him becoming my everything with time.

"It's crazy. I never would have thought—"

"Never would have thought what, babe?" River was back, all of his things in his arms. He dumped them on top of the bed, where we'd just had sex not that long ago, before bringing his toiletries into the bathroom, where we'd had sex in the shower before Stacy knocked on the door.

"That we'd ever get together," I said before he wrapped his arms around me and kissed my neck.

"Me neither."

"Okay, you two are gross. Thanks for the room," Stacy

said before walking through the adjoining door. "I'll be locking my side."

TWENTY MINUTES LATER, the three of us were riding the elevator down toward the bar for a classic American Thanksgiving meal.

I'd talked to my mom right before, and to my surprise, she hadn't made me feel guilty about not being able to get home. I thought River had had something to do with that.

When I had been video-chatting with her, he had shoved his face in the screen and introduced himself before saying a bunch of flattering things about me. I saw her eyes light up, and suddenly, all she cared about was when she was going to meet him in person, how long he'd been a pilot for, and what his mom was like in Miami. I thought she had started planning our wedding by the time we ended the call.

The elevator halted, the cage bouncing, and River reached for my hand and weaved his fingers with mine as we exited. Apparently, we were making a statement.

"How do you think Chad will react?" I whispered to

River and felt his grip on me tighten.

"Hopefully with a comment that won't make me want to hit him this time."

Before anything else was said, our group came into view. Along with a couple of additions from Stacy's flight—both pilots.

"Shit. You two really did hook up. I was joking. I think." Chad acted like nothing bad or untoward had occurred last night.

Maybe he didn't remember all the things he'd said. Or maybe he simply didn't care.

"Are you two a thing now? Is this really happening?" Carmella asked, her eyebrows wagging, but there was concern behind her gaze.

She didn't want me to get my heart broken.

I looked at River, letting him answer for us both.

"It's definitely a thing, and it's happening. Right, babe?"

My cheeks heated with the term of endearment, and I buried my head in his shoulder instead of saying anything in response.

You see, there were no guarantees when it came to

love. If you thought about it, most of the time, relationships didn't work out. They ended. Sometimes badly. But we always moved on, in search of the next person to give our heart to.

Whatever was going to happen with me and River, it was worth the risk.

River pulled out a seat for me, and I sat before he scooted it closer to the table and took the seat next to mine. His hand instantly found my thigh, and it stayed there, his thumb gently moving back and forth.

"What about when we're done being snowed in?" Chad asked, directing his question at my new ... whatever River was.

"What about it?" River responded.

"Will you two still be a thing when we go back to work? Or is this just a holiday fling?"

Chad actually wasn't trying to be an asshole with his questions. I could tell by the tone of his voice that he was just genuinely curious.

"This is the start of something real," River answered.

I bit my bottom lip to try to stop myself from smiling, but couldn't. I felt the grin take over my whole face.

Raul appeared with a big smile of his own even though I was sure he had to be tired. Other than one other bar employee that I'd only seen sporadically, I hadn't noticed anyone else helping him.

"Happy Thanksgiving, everyone," he said. "We've opened the buffet tonight, so you can have your classic holiday meal your way. The meat is turkey or ham. There are three different kinds of potatoes, two types of stuffing, steamed vegetables, salad, cornbread, fresh rolls, cranberry sauce, and apple pie for dessert."

"That's awesome," I said because I loved the idea of choosing our favorite foods, like we would if we were at home.

"I'll bring you some dinner plates, and then you can head over. Let me know what you'd like to drink, and I'll start making them. Except you." He pointed at Chad and laughed. "Joking, joking. But maybe not so many tonight, all right?"

Chad's face turned bright red, and this time, I knew it was because he was embarrassed.

"Yeah. Okay. Sorry about that."

Once our plates were filled and we were all seated

back at the table, I raised my hand in the air, getting the attention of everyone in the group.

"Do you think we could go around the table and say what we're thankful for? I know it's cheesy, but it was something my dad loved to do, and I'd love to carry on the tradition, if you guys don't mind."

"I love it." Carmella grinned. "I'll go first."

We all stared at Carmella, our respective drinks that we'd ordered from Raul held in the air while she spoke.

"I'm thankful for my family and for my work family. That's you guys." She winked. "I'm thankful that Sky doesn't hate River anymore and that River might actually settle down with a nice girl."

"Oh my God," I breathed out before taking a sip of my wine.

River kissed my cheek, completely unfazed. He loved the attention.

"Me next," Chad chimed in, and I held my breath, hoping he didn't say something inappropriate. "I'm thankful that you guys don't hate me after everything I said and did last night. And I'm thankful for ice cream and all the women it's brought into my life."

"What does that mean?" Stacy asked.

"You don't want to know," I said before rolling my eyes.

The other two pilots basically said that they were thankful for a good meal and that they didn't have to spend the holiday with their wives, pretending to like their cooking, and their in-laws. It was a shitty thing to say, but not really surprising. I felt like I'd seen and heard it all in this industry, and it had only been three years.

"I'm thankful I finally know the truth," Stacy said without elaborating further. Everyone else was in the dark, but not me or River. "Your turn, Sky," she added.

I looked around at the table, unsure of how much I wanted to share with the newcomers, but this had been my idea in the first place, so I couldn't *not* participate.

"I'm thankful for the snowstorm. It forced me to stay in this hotel instead of going home. Without it, I'm not sure this would have ever happened." I glanced at River, and if I was going to say more, it didn't matter because he started talking.

"I've never been more thankful for a storm in my life. Or for Chad being an asshole and hitting on Sky last night and making me see what I'd been denying for so long." He pointed at Chad, who raised his glass in acceptance of what he took as a compliment.

"I'm thankful for adjoining rooms." He gave me a wink before eyeing Stacy. "And women who are willing to listen and forgive. I'm thankful for our job. The people we get to meet. The places we get to go. But mostly, I'm thankful that my enemy has now become my lover."

He leaned down and started kissing me at the table, which erupted into cheers.

Oh my God, we're a freaking book trope.

When River broke the kiss, everyone was grinning, drinking, and digging into their meals.

"Happy Thanksgiving, Sky."

"Happy Thanksgiving, River."

"To Ocean and Star," Chad said, his glass held high in the air.

Even though no one else at the table, except Carmella, knew what the hell he was referring to, they all repeated the cheers anyway.

"To Ocean and Star!"

I looked at River, who said the toast at the same time I

did and smiled before taking a sip of his beer. Normally, I might have been worried or a little scared at how fast things seemed to be moving between us, but for some reason, I wasn't. And River didn't seem to be either.

Which should have been weird as well, but instead, it all felt right.

"After we eat, I'm taking you outside to play in the snow," River whispered in my ear.

I looked down at my clothes. "I'm not dressed for snow."

"No, you're dressed like we're back home. We never get snow in Florida," he said.

I realized this was more for him than it was for me. He just wanted an accomplice or someone to go with him.

"Fine, but when your fingers fall off and you can't fly the plane anymore, don't say I didn't warn you."

"You'd never let anything like that happen to me," he said, and in that moment, I had to agree that he was right.

The same way he'd protected me last night from what he deemed was a threat, he knew that I'd do the same for him. Me against the snow. I could see it now. I'd blow on it until it turned into water. Snow was no match for me and my hot breath. Try to hurt my man, and I'd melt you.

"What are you thinking about?" River crooked his head and gave me a look, and I knew I must have been making some kind of face.

"Just fighting the snow on your behalf." I shrugged my shoulders, and he pressed a kiss there.

"I thought you might be daydreaming about food again," he teased.

My mouth formed a smirk in response. I was surprised I hadn't started drooling.

"What are we going to bring back to the room? None of this is good cold." I waved a hand over our Thanksgiving meals.

"Mashed potatoes are okay cold. And the bread will be fine."

I wasn't convinced. Both of those sounded subpar, and I knew I'd be hungry later. For actual food.

"Raul will make me a pizza to go. Won't he?" I batted my eyelashes at River, and he brushed his thumb down my cheek.

"If he won't, I will."

"Who knew you were so sweet?"

"My mom," he quipped without taking a breath, and I laughed. "But the pizza's for both of us, babe. You're going to need the energy for what I have planned."

I dropped my fork, and it clanged loudly against my plate. I felt my cheeks flush, and I started waving a hand to fan my face. My body was already sore in places I hadn't realized could even get that way. I really needed to start stretching more. Especially if River was going to be in charge of my sex life. That man had moved my body into positions I'd never managed to get into before. At one point, I had sworn I was folded in half like a lawn chair while he railed into me.

Not that I was complaining.

I was just definitely going to need that pizza. And maybe a massage.

EPILOGUE

SKY

SEVEN MONTHS LATER

I HAD TO sit on my suitcase in order to get it closed. I was usually better than this, but I was also typically packing for work and not a tropical vacation with my boyfriend. River had insisted that we enjoy the spoils of our job and actually use our perks to go somewhere and relax.

We really did work a lot. And with our busy schedules and overtime requests, we didn't get to see each other as much as we'd like, even now that we lived together. Yeah, I had moved into River's condo in Miami a few months back. And, yes, it had been deemed quick by everyone around us, but River and I weren't into taking things slow.

Fast worked for us. Anything else felt uncomfortable and like we were forcing ourselves to follow someone else's rules for how we should live our lives. We both hated it and had realized pretty early on that we were doing things because we were *supposed* to, not because it was what we wanted or how we truly felt.

We wanted to live together, make dinner in our kitchen, make love on the balcony, and never spend our moments apart when we didn't have to. It was still insane whenever I thought back to how we had gotten here. I'd wasted so many years hating the man for no reason really when we could have been doing this the whole time instead.

Although we probably wouldn't have worked out before now anyway. When things were supposed to fall together, they seemed to do it without much effort. Timing was everything, and the two of us were no exception.

"Are you almost ready, babe?" He poked his perfect head through our doorframe before he started laughing. "What's happening here?" He pointed at the suitcase, damn well knowing that I couldn't get it zipped.

"I can't close it."

"That means you have too many clothes. I told you, bikinis and that's it."

Shaking my head, I narrowed my eyes at him, trying to fight off the smile that threatened to overtake my face. "I need to wear actual clothes in restaurants, River."

"Not if I don't let you leave the room to eat, you don't."

"Are you planning on keeping me hostage this whole vacation?"

"Damn straight." He stepped into our bedroom, picked up my body like I weighed nothing, and zipped up the suitcase with no effort. "There."

"You're so annoying."

"But you love me."

"I definitely do," I agreed, and in the next second, I was in his arms, my lips pressed against his.

Every time we kissed, I forgot the rest of the world existed. Everything faded away, and my knees felt like they were about to buckle. Thank God he always had the foresight to hold on to me. If he let go, I knew I'd fall.

"We need to go," he said with a crazy look in his eyes

before adding, "Just because we work for the airline doesn't mean they'll hold the plane for us."

We weren't even remotely close to being late or missing our flight. I didn't run behind. Professionally or personally. I was punctual, and my boyfriend was being weird.

"Okaaay," I said, dragging the word out. "I'm ready."

"Come on," he insisted before grabbing my suitcase and my hand.

We made a beeline for our front door like the condo was on fire, and I still had no idea why.

RIVER

I WAS COMPLETELY rattled and about two seconds from Sky asking what the hell was wrong with me and then bolting out of my grasp while she dumped me in the process. I kept telling myself to calm the hell down, take a deep breath—or twelve—and pull it together. But nothing worked. The diamond ring I had stashed in my carry-on with a note to security, begging them not to pull it out in front of her, were making me anxious.

What if they miss the note?

What if they open the box in front of her and blow my whole surprise proposal?

The last thing I wanted to do was ask the woman of my dreams to marry me in the fucking Miami International Airport. There was nothing romantic about that. Especially since airports were part of our jobs. What woman wanted to be proposed to at the office? None that I was aware of.

I started to sweat, just thinking about it.

"River?" Sky asked, her voice sweet and a little concerned.

"Yeah, babe?"

"Are you okay? Is something wrong?"

See? She knows something's up. Deflect, idiot.

"This is our first real vacation, and I don't want anything to mess it up. That's all." I really hoped she believed that. I stopped walking, leaned down, and pressed a quick kiss against her mouth.

"I'm excited too," she whispered, biting her bottom lip.

"I'd be more excited if you'd packed less clothes," I teased, wrapping an arm around her as we headed toward my car.

Reaching in my pocket, I pressed a button, and the trunk of my Audi sprang open. I wheeled both of our suitcases toward it and tossed them inside. I was heading to Barbados with my girlfriend, but I'd be coming home with my fiancée.

Unless she said no when I asked her.

Oh my God, what if she says no?

What if she isn't ready?

I started sweating again.

Why didn't anyone tell me how nerve-racking this whole thing was? It was like some well-kept secret that no guy ever talked about. Kind of fucked up, if you asked me.

She isn't going to say no, dummy.

She loves you.

You've talked about getting married a hundred times before.

Sky knew where we were headed, but she didn't know that I had rented us a private villa on the beach. We'd have an ocean view, three bedrooms, our own pool, and a private chef. I had gone all out for this trip. I wanted it to be perfect. She deserved nothing less, and I only planned on doing this one time.

One proposal.

One wedding.

One wife.

The past seven months with Sky had been truly life-changing. I had found my partner, the person I wanted to share everything with. She made all my days brighter, and I couldn't wait to come home to her whenever I landed.

It was something I'd always wanted, but wasn't sure I'd ever find. No one had made me feel this way before. My mother and siblings adored her. And vice versa. It was crazy how we'd come so far in such a short amount of time. From hating each other to not being able to live without one another.

A part of me had thought I might be a bachelor forever.

I couldn't be happier to be proven wrong.

By my little redheaded spitfire, who was currently sitting in my passenger seat with a smile on her face, completely clueless as to what was coming next.

All the good stuff. The best stuff. That was what was coming.

Right after she said yes to my proposal.

The End

Thank you so much for reading my Thanksgiving story! Writing this enemies-to-lovers with forced proximity was so much fun, and I hope you loved it!

All the FUN FOR THE HOLIDAYS books are out now—twelve complete stand-alone romance stories with holiday-based themes! And in case you're an audio lover, they're available in audio now as well for the first time ever. :)

Thank you so much for reading! Turn to the next page to see all the books I have available. There's a lot. You should read them all. LOL.

Other Books by J. Sterling

Bitter Rivals—an enemies to lovers romance

Dear Heart, I Hate You

10 Years Later—A Second Chance Romance

In Dreams—a new adult college romance

Chance Encounters—a coming-of-age story

THE GAME SERIES

The Perfect Game—Book One

The Game Changer—Book Two

The Sweetest Game—Book Three

The Other Game (Dean Carter)—Book Four

THE PLAYBOY SERIAL

Avoiding the Playboy—Episode #1

Resisting the Playboy—Episode #2

Wanting the Playboy—Episode #3

THE CELEBRITY SERIES

Seeing Stars—Madison & Walker

Breaking Stars—Paige & Tatum

Losing Stars—Quinn & Ryson

Flirting with Sunshine

Falling for the Boss

Tricked by my Ex

The Thanksgiving Hookup

Christmas with Saint

About the Author

Jenn Sterling is a Southern California native who loves writing stories from the heart. Every story she tells has pieces of her truth in it as well as her life experience. She has her bachelor's degree in radio/TV/film and has worked in the entertainment industry the majority of her life.

Jenn loves hearing from her readers and can be found online at:

Blog & Website:
www.j-sterling.com

Twitter:
www.twitter.com/AuthorJSterling

Facebook:
www.facebook.com/AuthorJSterling

Instagram:
@ AuthorJSterling

If you enjoyed this book, please consider writing a spoiler-free review on the site where you purchased it. And thank you so much for helping me spread the word about my books and for allowing me to continue telling the stories I love to tell. I appreciate you so much. :)

Thank you for purchasing this book.

Sign up for my newsletter to get emails about new releases, upcoming releases, and special price promotions:

NEWSLETTER

Come join my private reader group on Facebook for giveaways:

PRIVATE READER GROUP

facebook.com/groups/ThePerfectGameChangerGroup

www.ingramcontent.com/pod-product-compliance
Lightning Source LLC
Chambersburg PA
CBHW052144170626
46812CB00004B/1575